• • • • – –

"You right. What we did in them woods ain't just about killing. It's about what they used to do to us. For every man the KKK lynched, they could'a just shot him dead and kept it moving. But that wasn't their M.O. They chose to string 'em up and make a spectacle out of it. They was proud of it. They wanted people to see what happens when you step out of line. They took their hoods off and posed for pictures with the bodies. And what do you think they did with those pictures?"

Zahra had no idea.

"They made postcards out of 'em," Demon told her. "They was passing around racist postcards of dead black people like they was baseball cards, collecting souvenirs of our dead ancestors. I'm doing the same thing to them as they did to us. My video is an updated version of their postcards. Everybody with a cellphone is invited to our lynching party. But you think I went too far?"

"I didn't say that, David." In his eyes, she saw resilience as cold as steel. "I, I don't know..."

"Never forget what our true goal is," he said. "At the core, our group was created to let these people know that anything they do or *have done* to us can get done right back to them. The people we going after have a choice. They *choose* to join racist groups and plot attacks against our people. If that's the path they wanna go down, then they need to know that retaliation is likely, and retaliation can look like whatever we want it to. They think going to prison is the worst that can happen to them – or getting shot by the police and becoming a martyr for their cause."

He shook his head. "Nah. It's a lot worse things that can happen to them. We proved that tonight. When they see this video, they gon' get another opportunity to choose their path. I'm not taking the high road against people who have done my people wrong for centuries. Fuck 'em. Fuck 'em all. They gon' get what's coming to 'em, and they deserve every bit of it. *Nine bodies don't make a dent in the numbers they put up against us* – not even close. Anybody who think I went too far need to pick up a fucking book and do the math."

• • • • • •

TAKE ONE OF MINE 2

TAKE ONE OF MINE 2

KEITH THOMAS WALKER

*For Kyagn,
Much love and God bless!*
6/11/23

KEITHWALKERBOOKS, INC
This is a UMS production

KEITHWALKERBOOKS

Publishing Company
KeithWalkerBooks, Inc.
P.O. Box 690
Allen, TX 75013

For information write
KeithWalkerBooks, Inc.
P.O. Box 690
Allen, TX 75013

ISBN-13 DIGIT: 978-1-7356151-4-1
ISBN-10 DIGIT: 1-7356151-4-5
Library of Congress Control Number: 2022916432
Manufactured in the United States of America

Visit us at www.keithwalkerbooks.com

This book is dedicated to the memory of our martyrs. Unfortunately, there are too many to name. Most of them lost their lives before the days of hashtags.

MORE BOOKS BY KEITH THOMAS WALKER

Fixin' Tyrone
How to Kill Your Husband
A Good Dude
Riding the Corporate Ladder
The Finley Sisters' Oath of Romance
Blow by Blow
Jewell and the Dapper Dan
Harlot
Plan C (And More KWB Shorts)
Dripping Chocolate
The Realest Ever
Jackson Memorial
Sleeping With the Strangler
Life After
Blood for Isaiah
Brick House
Brick House 2
One on One
Brick House 3
Jackson Memorial 2
Backslide
Threesome
Backslide 2
Threesome 2
Election Day
Evan's Heart
Asha and Boom Part 1
Asha and Boom Part 2
Asha and Boom Part 3
Blurred Lines
Take One of Mine Part 1

NOVELLAS

Might be Bi Part One
Harder
Primal Part One
The Realest Christmas Ever
Hotline Fling

POETRY COLLECTION

Poor Righteous Poet

FINLEY HIGH SERIES

Prom Night at Finley High
Fast Girls at Finley High
Bullies at Finley High

Visit www.keithwalkerbooks.com for information about
these and upcoming titles from KeithWalkerBooks

ACKNOWLEDGMENTS

Of course I would like to thank God, first and foremost, for giving me the creativity and drive to pursue my dreams and the understanding that I am nothing without Him. I would like to thank my beautiful wife and my mother for always pushing me to be the best I can be. I would like to thank Janae Hafford for being the best advisor, supporter and little sister a brother could ever have.

I would also like to thank (in no particular order) Beulah Neveu, Deloris Harper, Denise Fizer, Michele Halsey Hallahan, Priscilla C. Johnson, Edwina Putney, Cathy Atchison, Lanita Irvin, Cynthia Antoinette Taylor, Jason Owens, Ramona Brown, Sharon Blount, BRAB Book Club, BSURE Book Club and Uncle Steven Thomas, one love. I'd like to thank everyone who purchased and enjoyed one of my books. Everything I do has always been to please you. I know there are folks who mean the world to me that I'm failing to mention. I apologize ahead of time. Rest assured I'm grateful for everything you've done for me!

CHAPTER ONE
LIKE FATHER LIKE SON

The militia, ominously named *Stormfront*, had close ties to the Oath Keepers and the Three Percenters, but the 19-member faction maintained autonomy in a northern region of North Dakota. Like the Three Percenters, Stormfront was founded on the principle that a small number of true patriots may one day have to take up arms to defend the country from a tyrannical government. With the emergence of Trump, the militia's anti-government rhetoric tempered, as they saw the disgraced president as their savior. Their resentment found a new target in Antifa and the Black Lives Matter movement. The violent protests following the death of George Floyd gave Stormfront a new yet familiar face to hate. But the paramilitary unit resisted the term *hate group*. Considering how much they loved their country, they were more of a *love* group. Just a jolly band of good-old-boys prepared to do whatever was necessary to make America great again and secure the existence of their people and the future of white children.

At eleven-thirty on a balmy Saturday night, Zahra and Demon were wide awake and equally determined to carry out the goals of their group. They plotted in a Holiday Inn Express, located in Devil's Lake, which was roughly an hour and a half away from Bottineau. Not all 19 members of Stormfront were currently holed up in their Bottineau bunker, but the bulk of them were there. They typically met at the bunker once a month and conducted training exercises in the isolated woods. Tonight, according to intel Demon had intercepted, they were there because they sensed a more sinister storm was on the horizon. They believed they could find safety in numbers.

The accommodations in the hotel room were modest. No bells or whistles. Comfortable enough for the vacationing couple Zahra and Demon appeared to be when they checked in earlier that day. They had not traveled to the state alone, but no other member of their group had checked in to the same hotel. The notoriety of the Ace of Spades had reached international infamy. It wouldn't do to have multiple people, all as black as spades, converge on a city where the population of blacks was a mere one percent. For this reason alone, this mission may have been too risky an undertaking. Head had other causes for concern. The computer guy sat safely behind his desktop in the group's Houston headquarters. Demon sat on the hotel bed and spoke to him with a throwaway cellular.

"Even if y'all make it up there," Head was saying, "we still don't know if they got the whole area boobytrapped. With all those trees, you know we didn't get good intel with those drones."

"I think we'll be ready for any boobytraps," Demon argued.

"You *think*? That's good enough for you – you *think*?"

"We train just as good as them."

"Yeah, but you on they home turf. I know you did your research on how the best military in the world thought they was just gon' roll through Vietnam like it wasn't shit. They got in that jungle and found out shit wasn't so sweet."

"Ain't you got that drone up now?" Demon asked.

"Yeah. I been watching it for an hour."

"And you said them heat signatures all together, bunched up underground..."

"Yes, they're all in the bunker. But that don't mean they'll be easy pickings. You seen those messages. I think all of 'em holed up like that is more dangerous than if they were spread out."

"And I think the opposite."

Demon's eyes were ice cold. He stared at Zahra, who stood before the bed, her eyes glued on his. She wore all black. Long sleeves, combat boots, tactical gear. Demon's attire was identical. Zahra's demeanor was unreadable, but if he had to guess, Demon would say she was as prepared for war as he was.

Head sighed in resignation. He said, "Two a.m.?"

Demon nodded. "That's right. That's go time."

"All three locations at the same time – you still think we can pull that off?"

"I know we can. The bunker is the only one I'm a little unsure about, but I'm more sure than unsure. We been done gave this job a green light, and I ain't calling it off – if that's what you trying to do."

"No, I ain't trying to call it off. Just want y'all to be careful. I know our soldiers are prepared, willing to die if need be. But that don't mean you have to send them storming up Bunker Hill."

Demon continued to stare into his woman's eyes. He didn't keep secrets from Zahra, but he was glad that she hadn't heard Head's comment.

"The aftermath of this is gonna make a lot of rednecks think twice about joining or staying in a militia," he said. "They women gon' tell 'em it ain't worth it. They got families, kids to feed."

"And some rednecks who never thought about joining are gonna see this as a reason to come together."

Demon hmphed at that. "Listen man, I ain't come all the way to Devil's Lake to listen to you play devil's advocate. This job was Cujo's idea. Remember? If you had reservations about it, you should'a taken it up with him a long time ago. I gotta get off this line. Got something to do before we head out."

Demon disconnected and took a moment to steel his emotions before rising from the bed, finally looking away from Zahra as he stepped past her. She followed him out of the bedroom. She did not ask what Head had said or if everything was alright. In the front room, Demon methodically checked two large duffle bags that were on the sofa. He had already checked them tonight and did not find anything amiss with their gear now. He zipped the bags closed a final time and approached two more bags that were on the floor next to the sofa. He dropped to his knees and unzipped the first. He checked his watch and then pulled a pair of work gloves from his back pocket, after determining they had time for this final step.

He removed a rope from the bag. It was pre-cut, measuring twenty feet. Zahra's knowledge of ropes was limited, but she knew this one was strong, not too thick, but sturdy. She watched as Demon selected one end and created two folds pointing in opposite directions. He then began to roll the slack around them into a coil. He tucked the remaining end into one of the folds and tightened the coil. It took less than thirty seconds to fashion the first noose.

Nothing Zahra was seeing was unexpected. She knew he had brought the ropes, and she knew what their purpose would be. But still... The dark history inexplicably intertwined with the noose made every one of her blood cells freeze and tremble. Somehow she managed to catch her breath as he rolled the first noose into a compact spiral and set it aside. He reached into the bag and selected another rope. Zahra's heart thundered as she approached him. She dropped to her knees as well. She pulled the second bag to her and watched him again, before slipping her small hands into a pair of manly gloves and attempting to fashion a noose of her own.

Other than Demon's instructions in the beginning – to "slide that last piece in there," and "make sure it's tight," they did not speak for the duration of the task. When they were done, they returned the ropes to the bags, but they weren't the same anymore. The innocent fibers had become something grisly.

Like the ropes, Zahra knew that after tonight, the Ace of Spades would never be the same. She did not voice her opinion on what they would become.

∞ ∞ ∞ ∞ ∞ ∞ ∞

At precisely 2 a.m., Tasha and Zulu breached the entrance of the first target's home in the rural town of Rugby, a 50-minute drive from the militia's Bottineau bunker. With a population of 2,500 and over ninety percent of the residents classified as white, this was another area where caution was crucial. The two-man team waited until an hour before go-time before they even considered entering the city limits. That didn't allow for much on-site surveillance, but they'd been monitoring the property for over an hour by way of a drone that sent a live video feed to Zulu's cellphone. The battery life for the average consumer drone was 22 minutes, but the drones Demon had invested in were fixed-wing and could remain airborne for up to two hours.

Even still, no amount of outside surveillance can fully prepare a soldier for what they might encounter once they enter a building. Creeping slowly down the darkened hallway of the two-bedroom flat, Zulu was alerted by a sound directly behind him. It was the unmistakable metallic clamor of a shotgun shell being chambered.

Someone had gotten the drop on him.

He stopped in his tracks and stood motionless. Ahead of him, the only light in the house illuminated from the kitchen, which was around the corner to the right.

A moment passed before the person behind him ordered him to, "Turn around. Do it slow."

Zulu was not relieved to hear that this was the son's voice. The boy was only midway through high school, but he was armed, and kids his age had proven to be just as dangerous as their gun-loving parents.

Before complying, Zulu told him, "I got a gun in my hand. You want me to put it down first?"

"Yeah," the boy said. "Put, put it down – *slowly* – and then turn around."

Though he had the upper hand, the teen's voice was laced with uncertainty. That was not necessarily a good thing. Zulu would've preferred if the finger on the trigger behind him was calm and steady. He bent and placed his pistol on the threadbare carpet. His Glock 19 was all black. With the silencer attached, it looked massive, much longer than his size 13 boots. He raised his hands chest high as he turned, moving slowly, as the voice had instructed.

When they were face-to-face – Zulu's covered by a ski mask, and the boy's features deathly pale – they sized each other up in the scant lighting. Compared to the boy, Zulu was a dark hulk. His bulk seemed to fill the whole hallway. The teen was two feet shorter and a hundred pounds lighter. If not for the shotgun, Zulu could've snapped his scrawny neck as easily as he could twist the top off a beer bottle. The boy was redheaded and hadn't begun to sprout any facial hair. Despite the late hour, he was dressed in workpants and a camouflage tee. His boots were rough and sturdy, similar to Zulu's. The barrel of the shotgun was trained on the center of the intruder's chest.

They stood no more than six feet apart. Zulu doubted if he could close the distance quickly enough to disarm the kid before he got off a shot. Even if the boy chambered a round of buckshot, it could be deadly at that range. If the boy had chambered birdshot, or even worse, a slug, fatality was certain. Since the son hadn't pulled the trigger yet, Zulu opted to stall for time.

"That's a big gun. You know how to use that thing?"

"Course I do. You heard me cock it, didn't you?"

"What you doing up so late? I know it's the weekend, but shouldn't you be in bed?"

"I stayed up waiting for you," the boy said, sneering now. "We knew you was coming."

Zulu's eyes moved from the pale blue eyes down to the shotgun. The boy was holding it at hip level with the barrel pointed upwards. His finger was firmly on the trigger.

"That's why you dressed like that?" he asked. "You stayed up waiting, ready to go to war?"

"I should kill you right now," the youngster quipped. "But I'ma let my dad do it. You broke in our house, *and* you armed. It's justifiable. Ain't nobody–"

The boy heard a sound behind him. Before his head could whip around to see what it was, Tasha walloped him with a collapsible billy club. The teen dropped like someone unplugged his power cord.

"*God damn*," Zulu muttered.

She'd hit him so hard, the blow sounded like a skull fracture.

"What took you so long?" he whispered.

"I didn't wanna come running," Tasha replied with the same hushed tone. Her outfit was all black, as was Zulu's. Only her eyes and mouth were visible through her ski mask. Their attire was identical to Demon and Zahra's, who should be taking care of business in Bottineau at that moment. "I could tell he was jumpy," she said. "He might'a pulled the trigger."

Zulu nodded. "You did good."

"Where his dad at?"

"Hell if I know." Zulu bent to pick up his weapon. He trained it down the hallway, in the direction he was headed before the target's son intercepted him. He looked back at the body on the floor. "You gon' get that?"

"Definitely not turning my back on a gunman," Tasha said as she bent to retrieve the shotgun. "Even if he is sleep."

"You sure he ain't dead?" Zulu asked, his eyes on the hallway ahead. "You cracked the shit outta that melon."

"Nah, he breathing."

Zulu was on the move again. He wondered why the father hadn't been alerted to the disturbance. The son wasn't whispering during their brief interaction, and when his body hit the floor, it sounded loud enough to wake up anyone in the house. The answer to that question became obvious when Zulu looked right at the end of the hallway and encountered the kitchen. In addition to the place being a mess, white trash dilapidation at its finest, the father proved to be the less disciplined man in the home. The middle-aged man was asleep at the kitchen table, amidst a mess of Taco Bell debris, a few dirty dishes, and an empty bottle of Jack Daniel's – Tennessee's finest whiskey. Zulu guessed the bottle had been full earlier that night.

He resisted the urge to send a bullet through the crown of the balding man's head. He couldn't have had an easier shot. The target was seated, leaning over the table, with his head resting on his arms.

Free kill.

But one of the fundamental tenants of the Ace of Spades was to let targets know they were about to die and why. Tasha entered the kitchen behind him and said the same thing that was on Zulu's mind.

"I doubt if we woke his drunk ass up he'd understand anything we're saying."

"Prolly not," Zulu agreed. "But I'm sho gon' try."

He moved deeper into the kitchen towards the sink. The drunk man did not stir as Zulu walked past him. With a gloved hand, Zulu cringed as he selected a dirty plastic cup from the sink. The bottom third of the cup was soiled with used chewing tobacco and the spit that came with it.

"They talk all that shit about us," he said as he used the faucet to fill the cup with water, "but I ain't never seen a nigga living like this."

Tasha didn't respond. She had the son's shotgun leveled on the sleeping man, who was snoring sporadically.

Zulu returned to her side on the opposite side of the table. From that distance, he tossed the water, cup and all, at the sleeping man's head. He thought the man would drowsily reach for consciousness when the water hit him, but the effect was quite the opposite. The target's head jerked up from the table, and he tried to get his body to respond similarly. That didn't work. Instead, the big man floundered comically, his arms and legs flailing, as if he thought he was drowning. He made it out of his chair and promptly fell to the floor, coughing and gagging.

He reached up and used the table to pull himself to his knees. It was then that he locked eyes with the two blacks dressed in black. Zulu had heard that traumatic experiences can sober a person up in a matter of seconds. He'd never believed that until he saw it happen that night. The target's hazel brown eyes registered shock, clarity, and then understanding. The rumor's he'd heard about this group were true. The warnings from his militia were not an overreaction. And he should've stopped drinking tonight after half a bottle, as his liver, kidneys and son begged him to do.

Nevertheless, he was defiant when he spat, "What the fuck you nigger spades doing in my house?"

Zulu grinned slightly, his pistol pointed at his head again. "You mean *Ace of Spades*?"

"No! Fucking *nigger spades*! You heard what I said, and I meant it!"

Zulu chuckled. "Damn. When I first came in here, I thought you was just some sloppy ass drunk. Didn't expect you to have balls like this. But it's hard to take you seriously, with all that shit on your face. You look fucking disgusting."

The target didn't bother wiping any of the goo from his spit cup off his face, even though some of it was dripping down to his eyes. Noticing the man was shooting glances towards the hallway, Zulu turned to see who was back there. Of course there was no one.

"What you looking for?" he asked, facing the target again. "You waiting for your ace in the hole to rush in and save the day with his shotgun?"

"This shotgun?" Tasha asked, cradling the weapon.

"Yeah, that one," Zulu said. "That what you looking for?" he asked the target. "You waiting for your son to come kill us nigger spades with his shotgun?"

"How he gon' do that if I got his gun?" Tasha teased.

Zulu couldn't help but laugh at that. "Let the man answer. He look like he dying to get something off his chest."

"Wh, where my boy?" the man stammered. "I swear if you touch one hair on his head..."

"Well, he didn't just *give* us his shotgun," Tasha reasoned.

"I will say he's a better soldier than you," Zulu added. "He was up, waiting, ready and alert. Had combat boots on, a hunting shirt. *That's* how you go nigga hunting. You don't get drunk and fall asleep at your post, leave your beloved son to defend the castle."

With that, Zulu finally got the look he wanted from the man. Now there was uncertainty, dread and fear. He may have been a piece of shit racist redneck, but he loved his son dearly, as most of them did.

"You, you didn't hurt him. Tell me he's alright. Colby!" he called down the hallway. "*Colby!* Can you hear me?"

"He can't hear shit," Tasha said coldly. "Your ears stop working when you dead."

They watched as every muscle in the man's soiled face went slack before hardening just as quickly. Faced with such news, his only recourse was to get his hands on the ones who took away the thing he cared about the most. He didn't care what happened to him afterwards.

But Zulu had already calculated the innerworkings of his tormented mind. He didn't allow the target to make it to his feet and attempt a lunge before he pulled the trigger. The first bullet caught him on the right side of the face. The second missed. Zulu casually walked to the downed man and ended him with two more head shots. This time both shots were true. With the silencer, the reports made less sound than popping the cork on a champagne bottle. Zulu retrieved a playing card from his pocket and tossed it on the corpse before tuning Tasha's way.

"You think of that on the spot?" he asked. "Telling him his son was dead?"

"Yeah. You liked it?"

He nodded. "It was masterful. You got a quick wit. I like working with you."

"Me too," she said. "Batman and Robin."

They left the kitchen and encountered the son in the hallway. His position had not changed. There was now a growing pool of blood under his head.

"He prolly gon' die," Zulu guessed. "If he got a skull fracture left untreated for who knows how long, ain't no way he'll make it."

"I didn't hit him as hard as you think," Tasha said. "I don't think he got a skull fracture. He gon' wake up with a headache and a lump on his head, but he'll be alright within a week."

"Hmph."

They stood over the body. Tasha gave Zulu a look before drawing her pistol. She watched his eyes and did not see dissent.

All he said was, "You know Cujo won't like that. I think Einstein said he's only fifteen."

Tasha knew the boy's age. She also knew Cujo would be opposed to what she was considering. "What about you?" she asked.

Zulu looked down at the boy, who appeared very vulnerable and innocent at the moment, like an injured fawn separated from its mother.

"I think he gon' grow up and hate niggas just like his daddy, probably even more so, after what happened tonight."

Tasha nodded. "That's what I think too."

She took a couple of steps back to avoid the blood splatter before duplicating the carnage Zulu had left in the kitchen.

TAKE ONE OF MINE 2

Like father, like son.

CHAPTER TWO
END OF TIMES

At 1:58 a.m., thirty-five miles from the Bottineau bunker, an Ace of Spades' warrior named Polo made a turn onto Railroad Avenue and entered the desolate town of Wolford. Unlike the other target locations, subtlety was not an option for this mission. Wolford boasted a population of a whopping 43 residents, which included only 17 households. It was here that 9 members of Stormfront chose to find refuge for the night. Polo knew they would be as prepared as they deemed necessary for a possible attack.

The cat and mouse game with the militia started a few weeks ago. Demon made contact with them on their official website, using a form they conveniently provided to recruit new members. When they responded to him, Demon urged them to disband. If not, he warned that they would face the full wrath of the Ace of Spades. With the rise of their group's notoriety, these types of threats were common. Demon wanted their enemies to know that they had been targeted, and they were never safe – not even on the internet. The success of this cyber trolling had yet to be determined, but in this case, Demon hoped the militia would heed his warning. Everyone understood that killing all 19 members was a tremendous undertaking.

But the militia did not back down. Whoever was responding to Demon on the internet said that they were not afraid. They were prepared to defend themselves. And if Demon really was from the nigger Spades, he was cordially invited to come to North Dakota and attempt to carry out his threat. They would love to meet him. It would save them the trouble of tracking him down.

Although Demon didn't give a timeline for his visit, Stormfront knew that the Ace of Spades was real, and they believed an attack was imminent. Only one member of the militia chose to fend for himself that night. If he had not made that decision, his son would not have died for his sins. The other eighteen members were evenly divided between the bunker and a two-story home in Wolford. The drone hovering over this location showed eight vehicles on the property and nine heat signatures inside the home. As Polo turned onto the last street and saw the house in the distance, he wondered just how prepared these men were. Were they merely waiting for any sign of trouble? Were they posted in the windows with assault rifles facing the street? Or did they take this opportunity of togetherness to have a house party – a good old-fashioned hoedown?

He hoped it was the latter.

At precisely 2 am, he increased speed for the final few blocks. If the element of surprise was not on their side, he believed the lightning quick blitz of their attack would garnish success. An armed soldier sat in each of the remaining seven seats of his Tahoe. All remained silent and focused. On the road behind them, another Tahoe followed with eight more determined murderers. This was the torch crew. Behind them, a third Tahoe raced towards the two-story house.

All three vehicles came to a stop, almost at the same moment.

A second later, all hell broke loose.

Twenty-four men sprang from the vehicles, all clad in black, all wearing ski masks. The torch crew carried Molotov cocktails. They lit them up as they ran, encircling the home. As soon as they tossed the firebombs, making sure to hit all doors and most ground floor windows, the assault teams lit the house up from all directions. Fire and ferocity crushed the stillness of the night, replacing it with the sound of war. The torch team raced back to their Tahoe and returned with more incendiary devices. More fire engulfed the home. More bullets. More screaming from inside.

The smell of petrol and gun smoke singed the shooter's nostrils.

On the third trip to their vehicle, the torch crew returned with assault rifles.

The men kept firing.

After thirty seconds of the onslaught, only three members of the militia managed to attempt to flee the blazing devastation. Two through the back door, one through a second-floor window. They were quickly mowed down the moment they emerged from the home. After thirty more seconds, Polo held up a gloved fist, and the shooting stopped. The men waited – not long – only long enough to listen for any signs of life inside the home. All they heard was the sound of the fire feeding itself, growing hotter and stronger by the second. There were no streetlights in the area, but the fire was so bright, every soldier was bathed in its florescence.

Polo gave the signal, and his teams raced back to their vehicles. Before following, he tossed a dozen playing cards onto the front lawn. Given the wrath of the fire, it was likely the cards would be consumed by the flames as it continued to spread across the property.

He hopped behind the wheel and decided that was okay.

By morning, there would be no doubt about what had occurred here and who was responsible. His only concern was that his men would make it safely out of the state, and the other two missions, which were currently underway, were equally successful.

∞ ∞ ∞ ∞ ∞ ∞ ∞

At the same moment Tasha and Zulu breached the entrance of the first target's home, and later decided to put an adolescent boy down, rather than allow him to grow up with hate in his heart, the third tactical team entered the wooded area surrounding the Bottineau bunker. Though there were just as many targets at this location, Demon only brought nine soldiers with him. Other than Zahra, who was known as Cleo to the rest of the group, all of his soldiers were men. They were all strong and capable, handpicked for the task at hand.

Though the moon was high, it was late June, and the foliage was in full bloom. The dense tree cover blocked the moon and star light from reaching the ground, which was a beautiful mess of vegetation, fallen tree branches and uneven terrain. Every member of Demon's team wore black. Over their ski masks, they wore helmets that were secured by chin straps. Affixed to the helmets were night vision goggles. Without the goggles, they wouldn't be able to see their hand one foot away from their eyes. With the goggles, the indiscernible forest shone clearly with a bright, greenish hue. Looking to his right and then left, Demon thought his squad was as impressive as any special ops group the US military ever put together.

During the planning stage of this mission, Zahra had asked him what a bunker complex was. That was two weeks ago. While seated in the computer room of their Houston headquarters, Demon pulled up an image on his laptop and showed it to her.

"This is a pretty big one," he'd told her. "Not sure if the one in Bottineau is like this, but it's gotta be big enough for all 19 members."

On the picture, Zahra saw a floor plan that included sleeping quarters, bathrooms and even a kitchen.

She knew Demon's intel was accurate, but she shook her head in disbelief.

"I don't get it. What they need this for? They think the country's gonna get nuked?"

"Maybe," Demon replied. "These militias have different ideologies, but they're all preparing themselves for the end of times. Stormfront believes something catastrophic is going to happen – soon, and they're preparing for it. That's why they go out in the woods and do their training. They got veterans teaching them military tactics, running drills. They low crawling under barbed wire, running up muddy hills, practicing their shooting. They always practicing their shooting."

"They think the 19 of them can take on the whole government?" Zahra asked.

Demon shook his head. "No. But they think if all the other militias around the country get active at the same time, and they start carrying out terrorist attacks, they'll be able to overthrow a corrupt government. In the midst of that, if the government *does* come after them, they'll hide out in their bunker. They could probably spend a month down there, maybe longer."

"If *you* know about their bunker, what makes them think the government doesn't know about it?"

Demon chuckled. "They determined, but I never said they were geniuses. Anyway, lately, what they really hoping for is a race war. All the militias against the government may not work – but all the whites in this country against the blacks... That's something they think will go their way. They know we got guns too. They see all the shootings we doing every day. But they think we not disciplined like them. They think blacks won't stand a chance if they roll up to our hoods and take tactical positions. They think they're more organized and better trained."

Zahra gave that some thought then asked, "What do you think?"

Demon shrugged. "Better trained? Compared to the average citizen, yeah they are. But the training isn't as important as the numbers. Whites make up sixty percent of the country. Blacks are less than fourteen percent. When you take out all the people who are too young or old to fight and factor in the number of whites who'd go against them – because they not racist – I think we'd be close to pulling even.

"But I'm not worried about a race war, 'cause that would turn into a civil war, and that's something these militias can't win – unless they get another Trump in office." He chuckled, but it was without humor. "But anyway, it's like I told you. What we doing ain't about winning a war. We can't kill every racist out there. Our crusade is to let them know that they can't keep fucking with us with impunity."

"*You take one of mine...*" Zahra said, her eyes deep and dark.

"Damn right," Demon said.

As they closed in on the Bottineau bunker, Demon gave a signal to put his team on high alert. They were mindful of threats that could include anything from boobytraps, armed guards and the regional wildlife. No one in Demon's team had ever seen a moose outside of television. He had warned them that a bull moose can reach a height of six feet at the shoulders and weigh more than a thousand pounds. There were plenty of moose in this area.

Thanks to their night vision goggles, they spotted their first targets near the bunker's entrance. The two men sat talking and smoking, as they might have done on a lazy Sunday evening on the porch of one of their homes. They both carried flashlights, which they used to scan the woods occasionally, but they did not appear to be leery of their impending doom. They were, however, armed with assault rifles, and they were in position to deliver a quick warning to the men inside the bunker if need be.

Demon held up his right hand and then closed it into a fist to halt the progress of his team. Everyone stood deathly still. He pointed two fingers towards his eyes and then held the same two fingers up before pointing in the direction of the guards. When he was sure everyone saw what he saw, he picked a soldier named Bubba to carry out the next step. He gave more hand signals to Bubba and then raised his rifle to a firing position, with the stock firmly against his shoulder. From that distance, the guards could not hear him as he whispered the countdown.

"One. Two..."

The muffled pops of their silenced rifles were perfectly timed. Zahra watched both guards drop simultaneously. Demon was immediately on the move again. If the men had not been instantly killed, one of them might be able to scream an alarm with his dying breath. But when they reached the bodies, they were both motionless. Blood had already begun to pool under them.

With his team now surrounding the bunker, Demon gave the signal to search for the ventilation system. It was not hard to find. The humming of the unit below led one of the soldiers to the exhaust vent. Demon headed that way, motioning for another comrade named Mustafa to follow him. All of the men carried gear of some sort, but Mustafa's bag was the heaviest. They knelt next to the vent, and Demon helped him remove the large duffle from his back. They placed it on the ground and unzipped it, revealing a ten-gallon air tank. Demon fed the hose from the tank down the exhaust vent and used his throwaway to send a text message to Head, instructing him to reverse the flow of the ventilation unit. As he waited for a response, he signaled for his team to don their gas masks. Everyone was geared up by the time Head responded to his text.

"Done"

Though he'd seen it a thousand times, Demon marveled at what the computer geek could do from as far away as Houston. Head was fond of saying, "Anything that's run by a computer can be run by *my* computer." In today's society, that applied to virtually everything.

Demon gave another signal to let his team know he was about to turn the valve on the air tank. When he did, there was an audible hiss that did not subside. The team held their places, listening to the hiss, wondering what they would find when they entered the bunker. Other than Demon, none of them knew exactly what was inside the air tank, only that it was not air, and depending on the size of the bunker, it could take ten minutes to incapacitate all of the men inside. They waited the full ten minutes before converging on the bunker's entrance.

Bubba pulled the door open, while two soldiers trained their weapons on the opening. There was no need. No one inside the bunker stirred. From her vantage point, Zahra saw the unconscious, or possibly lifeless, body of one of the militiamen lying near the entrance. Behind him, she saw the foot of another downed man.

"We good," Demon said, speaking aloud for the first time in the past hour. "Let's make this quick."

Everyone knew what had to be done. No one voiced disapproval. It took ten minutes to drag all of the men out of the bunker, including the two they shot, towards the trunk of twin elm trees. Zahra hurried over with the duffle bags filled with ropes – which weren't merely ropes anymore. Her stomach twisted when Demon fastened the noose around the first pale white neck. The man was not dead. Most of the militiamen were, but she counted three that were unconscious and still breathing. The morality of what was about to transpire would weigh on some of their souls for months, even years – if they managed to live that long.

Demon tossed the free end of the noose over one of the strong tree branches. Three men waiting on the other side quickly hoisted the body until the man's feet dangled two feet above the ground. Though the target was alive, he did not struggle as he hung to death. He succumbed peacefully.

Staring up at his ghastly face, what Zahra saw was anything but peace.

When all nine men were hung, everyone stepped back as Demon readied his phone for the video. Zahra provided illumination with a flashlight. Her heart thundered. Her blood felt like ice water. What she was looking at, what they'd done, was beyond horrendous. The beautiful trees, now adorned with gruesome jewelry, could not have looked more foul if Satan himself had done this. Two trees. Nine lifeless bodies hanging. The militiamen were red and purple about the face. Some were foaming at the mouth. Some had soiled their pants. Their eyes bugged grotesquely. Their necks were stretched surreally at irregular angles. Zahra could not look away.

She held her flashlight and followed behind Demon as he recorded his video.

He recorded for a full minute before giving the final order for this mission.

"Alright. We did good. Let's get outta here."

Zahra turned off her flashlight, but with her goggles, she could still see everything clearly. She was grateful for the mask and helmet gear that hid her expression.

Knowing what you're going to do and actually doing it are two different things.

Her grandmother used to tell her that.

Those words had never rang so true.

She turned and walked solemnly with her group, who were all following their leader, who happened to be her man.

CHAPTER THREE
STRANGE FRUIT

After the missions, most of the teams involved headed to the group's tactical point in Wyoming. It was a nine-hour drive. The following day, they would catch flights to Houston or other tactical points across the country to carry out more missions. There was always much work to do. Zahra and Demon rode together in a black-on-black Charger, his preferred mode of transportation for their operations.

While she drove the first leg of the long drive, Demon made several calls. Most were to check in with the other soldiers who'd been active in North Dakota that night. The last call was to Einstein, the second half of their team of computer wizzes.

"I was never doubtful that y'all could pull this off," Einstein stated when he answered the phone. "But at the same time, I'm a little surprised that y'all did it."

"You ain't the only one," Demon commented. "Some of the guys who participated are surprised too."

And some of the girls, Zahra thought as she listened in on the call, her eyes on the dark, nearly deserted freeway.

"I'm about to send you the video," Demon said. "How long do you think it'll take you to put it together."

"Not long, no more than thirty minutes. You, are you sure you want me to do it? You haven't changed your mind?"

"No. I know what's gonna happen when it goes out, and I'm ready for it. *We're* ready for it."

As she listened to him, Zahra wondered, not for the first time, if he was including people in the *we* category who would actually disagree with his assertion.

"You don't have to rush," he told Einstein. "We'll be on the road till noon. By then everyone should know what happened in Wolford and Rugby. At ten o'clock, make the call to report the bodies at the bunker. I want all of that on the news before the video comes out. I'm sending it now."

"Gotcha," Einstein said. "I'll get to work on it, and I'll make the call at ten."

∞ ∞ ∞ ∞ ∞ ∞ ∞

With Demon driving the last leg of the trip, he encouraged Zahra to get some sleep. She could not. Every time she closed her eyes, she saw the bodies hanging from those trees, those tormented hanging mouths, so she kept her eyes open.

The Wyoming tactical point was one of many such locations strategically established throughout the country. It was not as large as their Houston headquarters, but with two floors and six bedrooms, it was large enough to accommodate most of the group members who chose to spend the night there. On this day, that included half of the men and women involved in the North Dakota missions, which meant a dozen of them had to make a pallet on the floor. None of them complained about this. They'd been up most of the day before the missions and another nine hours on the road to Wyoming. Most had already fallen asleep by the time Zahra and Demon entered the home through the garage at a little after 12 pm.

In the kitchen, they were greeted by several soldiers who had been waiting dutifully. This group included Zulu, Tasha, Bubba and Polo. They congratulated each other on their success and discussed details about the missions that were better communicated face-to-face. It was then that Demon first learned about the teenager Tasha and Zulu made the decision to terminate. Demon had proclaimed, more than once, that he was willing to kill a child if such an act was necessary to achieve their goals. But in the four years the group had been active, neither he nor any other member had ever harmed a child – until tonight.

A sense of foreboding fell upon the kitchen as the occupants waited for Demon's response.

"You right," he told Tasha, "about that boy growing up to hate niggas more than his dad. Y'all also right about Cujo not liking it. But that's not something you have to worry about. I'll take whatever heat comes from this. I don't think anyone will be thinking about that boy, once we release the video."

With the mention of the recording, another hush fell upon the group.

Zulu spoke up first. "You got the video? Is it finished?"

"Einstein sent me a rough draft," Demon replied. "I gotta make a few tweaks, and then it'll be ready. If you wanna wait up, I should be done in about ten or fifteen minutes."

Though Tasha's eyes were red and ringed with fatigue, she told him, "I'ma be up. Send it to me as soon as you're done."

"Yeah, me too," Zulu said.

"I might pass out before you finish," Polo said, "but send it to me too."

Demon nodded. "Alright." He left the kitchen and noticed the dozing bodies on the couch and floor of the living room. He looked back and asked Zulu, "All the bedrooms upstairs taken?"

"Naw," Zulu said. "We saved you one. We know you got work to do."

Zahra was not surprised to hear that. By his own admission, Demon only had ten to fifteen minutes of *work* to do. And if need be, he could have done it in the kitchen. She knew that they'd saved a room for him because although their group had no official leader, Demon was generally considered the man in charge. Good soldiers always make sure their leader is taken care of.

He and Zahra headed upstairs and found one bedroom empty and in pristine condition.

∞ ∞ ∞ ∞ ∞ ∞ ∞

Demon didn't rush to complete the video, but it only took him ten minutes to put the finishing touches on it. He sent the hard file to Einstein, and then used his phone to share it with the soldiers they'd encountered downstairs. Though she'd participated in creating the clip, Zahra waited anxiously, knowing that what they'd recorded in the Bottineau woods was much different than what he planned to offer the internet. He motioned for her to sit on the bed with him, and then he placed his laptop in her lap. He pressed play in Windows Media Player.

Zahra took a deep breath. When she blew it out, she thought she was prepared for what she was about to see.

She was not.

The video began with legendary jazz singer Billie Holiday, also known as Lady Day, on stage. Zahra could tell the footage was old, and not only because it was black and white. Behind the singer was a piano player, a black man, who wore glasses. The audience applauded, a prelude to what would be a historic live performance. When the applause died down, the singer stood stoically before speaking.

"And now a lil' tune written especially for me... *Strange Fruit.*"

The pianist began to play.

The music was somber. Zahra vaguely recognized the tune, but she hadn't heard it in years. She didn't think she'd ever seen this performance. Billie Holiday looked like it pained her to begin the song. It appeared as if she was currently witnessing the horror encapsulated in the upcoming lyrics, rather than looking upon an adoring crowd. She began to sing. Her voice was beautifully poignant.

"*Southern trees bear a strange fruit. Blood on the leaves and blood at the root. Black bodies swinging in the southern breeze. Strange fruit hanging from the poplar trees...*"

The music was simple. Holiday's expression was anything but. Zahra's heart bled for her.

Gradually darkness filled the screen, until only the singer's face and shoulders remained. This image slowly moved to the lower right corner. Another image appeared in the forefront. This was the video Zahra and

Demon had recorded. She saw the hanging white men. The resolution was startling. The men were all dead, as ghoulish as she remembered, with their tongues lolling, blood dribbling from some of their mouths. In the bottom corner, Billie Holiday remained visible. She continued to sing.

"Pastoral scene of the gallant south. The bulging eyes and the twisted mouth. Scent of magnolias, sweet and fresh. Then the sudden smell of burning flesh."

Zahra was enthralled. Holiday crooned as the cameraman walked slowly around the bodies, making sure to get longshots and closeups of the dead white faces.

"Here is a fruit for the crows to pluck. For the rain to gather, for the wind to suck. For the sun to rot, for the tree to drop."

As she reached the last line of the song, the video effects reversed. The dead bodies faded to black, and the original video of Holiday regained the center screen.

"Here is a strange and bitter crop."

With the last word, Holiday relinquished the composure she'd been struggling to maintain throughout the song. Though melodic, the last word was elongated, dragged out like a blood curdling scream. Her expression matched this effect. She threw her head back and belted the word *crop* for almost five seconds. Once again, the crowd applauded, while the singer resumed the stoic posture she had at the beginning of the video.

The screen went black, and then a solitary playing card appeared. It was the ace of spades. It remained on the screen for a few silent and ominous seconds, and then the video ended. This was Demon's vision, his masterpiece. Zahra understood what she'd seen and why her man was adamant about creating it.

But she was torn.

Demon took the laptop from her and closed it. He set it aside, and then he began to speak.

"Between 1877 and 1950, forty-five hundred people were lynched in the United States. That doesn't count all the black people who were gunned down in the streets, like dogs. I'm talking about just the *documented* lynchings, where the victims were hung up for the world to see. And that's *after* slavery ended. Do you know how many blacks were lynched *during* slavery?"

Zahra shook her head. Her mouth was dry, her soul pained. She stared at him, longing for the knowledge he possessed, appreciating the time he took to be her teacher and mentor.

He told her, "I don't know either. Nobody took the time to keep up with it back then. And I'm sure the forty-five hundred is a low count. Do you know why it was important for me to make this video? I mean, do you *really* understand what motivates me?"

Zahra wished she could respond positively to that question, but the truth was, Demon was, and would probably always be, mysterious, even to the woman he shared a bed with.

She told him, "I think I do. You wanna send a message..."

He nodded. "When this video goes out, on Facebook, Twitter, Instagram, they'll shut down the accounts that posted them, probably within a matter of minutes. But it won't matter. Millions of people will have seen it by then. A lot of those people will download it and repost it. Putting Billie Holiday on it makes it even more powerful. Seeing her sing about black lynchings with them white bodies on the screen, that's the best part. This is the most powerful thing I've ever done."

Though Zahra agreed with him, she sighed before saying, "But what about the negative attention it's gonna bring us? That's what our people are worried about. I don't think they're ready for this."

"We already decided to bring attention to ourselves," Demon argued. "We decided that when we voted on leaving the ace of spades after our missions."

"No..." She shook her head, frowning. "This is different. This ain't just killing some racists. This... This is way worse. I think it's some people out there who don't like what we doing, but they can understand it a little, like the white people who was down with the Black Panthers when they were talking about killing police – *pigs*. But what we did tonight – that wasn't just killing. They was already dead when we did that to them. I mean, most of 'em were."

"You right. What we did in them woods ain't just about killing. It's about what they used to do to us. For every man the KKK lynched, they could'a just shot him dead and kept it moving. But that wasn't their M.O. They chose to string 'em up and make a spectacle out of it. They was proud of it. They wanted people to see what happens when you step out of line. They took their hoods off and posed for pictures with the bodies. And what do you think they did with those pictures?"

Zahra had no idea.

"They made postcards out of 'em," Demon told her. "They was passing around racist postcards of dead black people like they was baseball cards, collecting souvenirs of our dead ancestors. I'm doing the same thing to them as they did to us. My video is an updated version of their postcards. Everybody with a cellphone is invited to our lynching party. But you think I went too far?"

"I didn't say that, David." In his eyes, she saw resilience as cold as steel. "I, I don't know..."

"Never forget what our true goal is," he said. "At the core, our group was created to let these people know that anything they do or *have done* to us can get done right back to them. The people we going after have a choice. They *choose* to join racist groups and plot attacks against our people. If that's the path they wanna go down, then they need to know that retaliation is likely, and retaliation can look like whatever we want it to. They think going to prison is the worst that can happen to them – or getting shot by the police and becoming a martyr for their cause."

He shook his head. "Nah. It's a lot worse things that can happen to them. We proved that tonight. When they see this video, they gon' get another opportunity to choose their path. I'm not taking the high road against people who have done my people wrong for centuries. Fuck 'em. Fuck 'em all. They gon' get what's coming to 'em, and they deserve every bit of it. *Nine bodies don't make a dent in the numbers they put up against us* – not even close. Anybody who think I went too far need to pick up a fucking book and do the math."

She reached for his hand and cradled it in her lap. It was unlikely that her compassion could quell the fire raging in his heart. She stared deeply into his eyes and spoke softly.

"David, I'm with you. You right. I support you, one hundred percent."

Surprisingly, her compassion did seem to lower his temperature.

He told her, "I know you just saying that. It's okay to be worried about what's gon' happen when this goes out."

"I'm never worried when I'm with you." There was no question as to whether she truly meant that.

"That's good," Demon said. "Because there will be hell coming our way in a few hours. You should try to get some sleep. We got a flight to catch at four."

Zahra checked the time. It was twelve-thirty. Given the drive time to the airport and Demon's tendency to get there at least an hour before the flight, she'd be lucky to nap for an hour and a half. That was just as well. Despite her fatigue, her mind was too frazzled to switch it off so easily.

Rather than sleep, she lay with her man, enjoying their closeness as he spooned with her from behind. She continued to see the dreadful hanging bodies when she closed her eyes. Now, the dead men were accompanied by Billie Holiday's hauntingly beautiful song, which played over and over in her head like a mantra. Keeping her eyes open did not make the visions disappear completely, but it helped.

She stared at the wall on the other side of the bed for what felt like an eternity until Demon stirred and pulled away from her. She turned over and saw that he was seated on the side of the bed, checking his phone.

He looked back at her and said, "It's time to go, babe."

It didn't appear that he'd gotten any sleep either.

Zahra got out of bed and headed for the bathroom for a quick shower. She resisted the urge to reach for her phone. She knew that the news she'd find there would have her completely caught up. She wouldn't be able to tear herself away, so they could get ready to leave.

CHAPTER FOUR
REVERBERATIONS

On the way to the airport, Zahra found social media ablaze with news of what they'd done in North Dakota. The Ace of Spades was the top hashtag on Facebook and Twitter. Zahra scanned the posts furiously, eager to check the pulse of the nation. Not surprisingly, most were appalled by what they'd seen and heard. Demon was equally interested. He asked Zahra to read some of the posts aloud as he drove.

"*They crossed the line,*" she read as she scanned. "'*They're calling for a race war...*' '*It's them versus all of us now. They're waging war against America...*' '*Killing kids crosses the line...*' '*They burned all those people...*' '*The video is disgusting...*' Some of them say they have the video," she reported. "But all the links I click on don't have it. I see a lot of screenshots, though. A ton of people have seen it."

"Head on over to black Twitter," Demon suggested. "Curious to know how our people feel about it."

"*Black Twitter?* How do I get to that?"

"It's just an expression," he said grinning.

Zahra didn't find the humor in any of this. "I, um…" Scrolling. "Okay, I found a black guy. He got almost half a million followers. He says, '*Given the racially charged atmosphere in our country right now, it's irresponsible and inconceivable that this group would do this. Don't get it twisted. Don't think that because this group is supposedly going after the people you believe are your enemies that the Ace of Spades should be considered our heroes. These people are making things much worse.*' A lot of people like his post."

Demon nodded. Zahra couldn't tell if he was bothered or not.

"Some people are saying they support us," Zahra informed him. "They getting a lot of hate, though. This one here says, '*White people been doing stuff like this to us for years. They got what they deserve.*' The comments under it are going back and forth: '*How can you say that? No one deserves to die for something they weren't directly responsible for.*' '*You wouldn't say that if it was your son killed for no reason.*' '*You're gonna get what you deserve one day too.*' '*Fuck 'em. I hope they kill* **more** *whites…*' It's all over the place, but from what I see, there's more people against us than on our side."

"That's what you're supposed to see," Demon said. "It's not *PC* to come out and say you support something like that. People on the internet care too much about their followers; they not trying to lose half of 'em with one tweet. Go to some real news. I wanna hear what the major networks are saying."

"Okay," Zahra said, backing out of Twitter. "You want conservative or liberal?"

"Don't matter."

"The story's on the home page everywhere," Zahra said, scanning her phone. "Here's, uh... Okay, I have a video from CNN. They did a story on it this morning..."

"CNN is not real news. But that's okay. Go head and play it."

"Want me to find something else?"

"No, it's fine."

She held the phone up, so Demon could steal glances at the video while he drove.

"It is with great shock and sorrow that we open today with news of a tragedy that has struck our nation's heartland," the reporter began. "Nineteen men and one teenager were brutally murdered last night in one of the most heinous acts of terror this country has ever seen. We have Sheldon Traylor at the scene of one of these horrific murders in the woodlands of Bottineau, North Dakota, a small town approximately ten miles from the Canadian border. Sheldon, we're told this particular crime scene is the most notable – not only because of the condition these bodies were found in, but also because the killers recorded a video at this location…"

The camera shot was divided evenly between the anchorman in the studio and a reporter who was outside in a wooded area. Zahra had been at these woods less than twenty-four hours ago, but they looked a lot different in the daylight. Despite the presence of crime scene investigators in the background, the area was less ominous and foreboding.

"That's right, Aaron," the on-scene reporter said. "Few words can describe the *atrocity* local law enforcement agents encountered when they were lured to this area this afternoon by an anonymous 9-1-1 call. By then, police had already responded to two other emergency calls, one in Rugby and the other in Wolford. At the Wolford location, the police responded to reports of gunfire. When they arrived, they found a two-story home engulfed in flames. After extinguishing the blaze, it didn't take long to determine that something sinister had occurred there. The police discovered three bodies outside of the home and later recovered *six more bodies* from inside the smoldering residence. The cause of death for all of those individuals has not been determined, but it is believed that they all died by gunfire.

"At the Rugby location, police discovered two more bodies. This time it was a father and son. The police have not released the identity of these victims, but they have informed us that the man and his son were murdered, and they describe these killings as *execution style*. That brought the number of dead from last night's carnage to *eleven*."

"This is truly heartbreaking," the reporter in the studio quipped. He appeared genuinely distressed.

"Aaron," the on-scene correspondent continued, "the police informed me that they had not fully processed the first two crime scenes when they were called to this third location in Bottineau. As horrible as the first two scenes are, it did not prepare them for what they would find here. In these woods directly behind me, police say *nine more men* were found dead. If not for the fact that a video of these murders has been circulating throughout social media, the police would not have released details about the condition in which these victims were found. But at this time, they have confirmed that the video footage on the internet is accurate. These men were in fact *hung from trees*. That brought the total number of victims from last night's mass murders to *twenty*."

The reporter in the studio shook his head, as if hearing this for the first time. "Sheldon, for all of this to occur on the same evening is truly disturbing."

"It is," the second journalist agreed. "Not only did these killings occur on the same night, but investigators have gathered evidence that leads them to believe they all occurred at approximately the same time. This was certainly a coordinated attack."

"Sheldon, in the video that is circulating online, a group that has become notorious for these types of murders has taken credit. At this time, have the police confirmed that the *Ace of Spades* is responsible?"

"Aaron, I did ask the investigators for that information. From past reporting, the group known as the Ace of Spades leaves a calling card at the scene of their crimes. At this time, the detectives here are declining to say whether an ace of spades playing card was left at any of these crime scenes. If we are to take the grisly video at face value, not only is the Ace of Spades responsible, but they may be attempting to justify their actions. But I would ask viewers to reserve judgement on who is responsible until the investigators here in North Dakota have made that determination."

"If you are just joining us," Aaron said, "the video we are referring to was first posted to several social media sites at twelve o'clock central time today. In the video, someone recorded what appears to be the murder scene in the wooded area of Bottineau, North Dakota. Included in the video is footage of Billie Holiday singing *Strange Fruit,* a song about lynchings, which was recorded in 1939."

"Aaron, I would like to ask our viewers to avoid watching the video we're discussing. For journalistic purposes, I had to watch it. If it was created by the Ace of Spades, it is not likely to have the intended effect. I have not heard from anyone, either professionally or on social media, who believe that because lynchings occurred in our nation's past, this group is justified in carrying out the crimes that were perpetrated against the people of North Dakota. The only thing these 19 men had in common is their affiliation to a group called *Stormfront*. And while Stormfront is known to expound right-wing ideologies, there is no documented evidence that they have ever committed any *racial crimes*, which is usually a qualifier for the type of people the Ace of Spades chooses to victimize."

Zahra backed out of the video. She felt sick to her stomach. She waited a few beats, hoping Demon would offer a full-throated rebuttal to the news segment.

But he only said, "Looks like we got their attention."

Zahra thought he'd add more to that statement, but he just kept driving.

She didn't say anything either.

∞ ∞ ∞ ∞ ∞ ∞ ∞

They arrived at the Houston headquarters at 8 pm. This was the first home Demon brought Zahra to over a year ago, when she made the decision to give up the life she'd known and follow him and his band of revolutionary murderers. Since then, the headquarters had been the closest thing she'd known to a home. It always felt good to return there after their missions. Today was no different.

In the front room, they were greeted by Cujo, Einstein and Head. The computer guys were instrumental in achieving much of the group's success. Though neither of them had pulled the trigger since their first murder, a rite of passage that was required for all members, Zahra didn't think very many of their missions would be possible without their hacking skills. The third man in the room was once Demon's right-hand man. The two didn't see eye to eye very often these days, but everyone considered Cujo the second leader of the group. Knowing Cujo didn't like this deferment, Demon chose to see their leadership as a shared responsibility.

He and Zahra greeted the three men. She was not surprised to see that Cujo's demeanor was dark and distant. She'd seen this look before, most notably on the first day she came to this house. At that time, Cujo objected to Demon adding so many new faces to the group. Before even meeting her, Cujo had decided that he didn't trust Zahra. Tonight, his ire was directed at Demon, rather than the woman they knew as Cleo. That didn't make Zahra feel any better.

Without preamble, Cujo said, "I called a meeting for tomorrow. So far, all but a few members have confirmed they will attend."

Given the stretch of their group, full member meetings were rare. Demon didn't bat an eye. "That's cool. I kinda expected you'd want to do that. But you and me should discuss things first, so we'll be on the same page."

That was the politically correct response, but Zahra found it almost laughable. These two were rarely on the same page.

"That's fine," Cujo said.

"What time is the meeting?" Demon asked.

"One o'clock."

"Good. That means we don't have to have our talk tonight. I'm bone tired. I'll get with you tomorrow before the meeting."

Cujo hesitated. It was clear he wanted to get something off his chest right then and there. But he didn't push it. "Alright. That's fine."

"Anybody else here?" Demon asked before heading upstairs.

"Yeah, a few people."

"Zulu and Tasha?"

Cujo nodded, his eyes burning. "Yeah. They upstairs."

"Alright," Demon said. "We gon' head up and get ready for bed. See y'all in the morning."

With that, he walked past the men, headed for the stairway.

Zahra was right behind him.

Upstairs, they dropped their things off in one of the bedrooms before Demon headed out again.

"You can go ahead and get settled in," he told her. "I wanna holler at Tasha and Zulu right quick."

"I wanna go too," Zahra said. "If they got here before us, I know Cujo had something to say to them. I wanna know what it was."

"Yeah. That's exactly what I was thinking."

They found their friends in separate bedrooms. Although Zulu and Tasha were as thick as thieves when it came to mission assignments, they were not a couple. After exchanging pleasantries, Demon asked them to come to his room for a brief conference. He closed the door behind them and cut to the chase.

"What happened when y'all got here? Cujo says we're having a meeting tomorrow. Y'all know what he wants to talk about?"

With the door closed, Zahra couldn't help but feel as if this little sidebar was crossing a line. They weren't plotting against Cujo, per se, but discussing him behind his back had an underhanded feel to it.

"I don't know what the meeting is about," Zulu said. "But I know he doesn't like that we killed that boy. He asked us about it when we got here. He wanted to know if it was necessary. Didn't seem like he liked our answer."

"Did you tell him I gave the okay for that?" Demon asked.

Zulu shook his head. "I didn't want to say that before talking to you first."

"But I told you I would take the heat for it."

"I know, but you didn't say to tell him you gave the okay. I didn't want to put your name in it without telling you I was gonna do it first."

Demon understood that. He sighed and shook his head. "Alright. Well, what about y'all? Are y'all okay with it?"

Tasha told him, "I'm the one who pulled the trigger. At the time, I felt like it was the right thing to do. But after seeing all that stuff on the news, and the way Cujo was acting when we got here, I don't know how I feel no more."

"That's okay," Demon said. "That means you got a conscious, which is a good thing. Look, I know that what happened last night was hard. Nobody ever wants to be put in that position. But your reason for taking that kid out was a good one. Not only was he a witness – and we ain't never left no witnesses behind – but that boy would've tried to avenge his father one day. One way or another, he wasn't gon' rest until he got even. That prolly would'a meant him killing some random black face. What you did prevented that, so ain't no need to feel bad about it."

Seeing they weren't convinced, he added, "Emmett Till was fourteen years old when they lynched him. They tortured him in a barn for who knows how long before they finally put a bullet in his head. Compared to him, what you did last night was damn right merciful. That white boy had no idea what hit him when you knocked him out, and he felt no pain when you finished him off. Motherfucker got off easy, as far as I'm concerned."

Tasha nodded.

"Any soldier that ever been in a *real* war knows that war ain't pretty," Demon stated. "I appreciate y'all. And like I said before, if anybody wanna come at you for what happened to that boy, I'm ready to answer for it. I wish they would come to me with that shit. Anyway, y'all try to get some sleep. I'll see you in the morning."

∞ ∞ ∞ ∞ ∞ ∞ ∞

After all they'd been through in the past 48 hours, all Demon had said to her and all he'd say to the others, Zahra couldn't wait to get her man alone that night. She couldn't explain why his knowledge and leadership was so attractive to her, but it was. Even seeing him in action at Bottineau, the way he'd led his team to string up those bodies... Everything about him was endearing. She longed to love him as much as he loved his people – not only the people in their group, but all of his people with dark skin who had been persecuted in this country since its inception.

After showering, they climbed into bed together. Despite the weariness in his eyes, Demon was still looking through his phone, rather than seizing the opportunity to get some rest. Zahra rose from the bed and strolled across the room to lock the door and turn off the lights. She rarely slept nude at their headquarters and tactical points. Tonight, her succulent brown flesh was enticing enough to make him set his phone aside. He stared at her bare ass and the glimpse of her breast that was visible from that angle.

After locking the door, he told her, "Wait," when she reached for the light switch.

She hesitated, her smoky eyes on his.

He told her, "Turn around."

Zahra did so, exposing herself fully. She felt vulnerable as his eyes moved up and down her frame, igniting small fires in her nipples and between her legs.

When his carnal, ocular desires had been gratified, he told her, "Okay, you can turn 'em off."

But Zahra had a change of heart. The look in his eyes filled her with erotic confidence. She knew Demon liked to watch her. She liked to watch his eyes enjoy every bit of her. She returned to the bed and peeled the sheets back. He wore only a pair of boxers, which he quickly shed. His eyes moved from dark orbs to her puckered lips as she crawled onto the bed and immediately took him into her mouth. He sucked air between his teeth as the warm wetness titillated his sensitive nerve endings, flooding him with a pleasure so powerful he was rock hard within seconds. She rode his wave of ecstasy with her mouth and her hands while he watched her, and she watched him marvel at the spectacle she provided.

He couldn't resist the urge to bring his hands to her face. His touch invigorated her, loosened a floodgate between her legs. She felt her clitoris pulsate as she licked and sucked him deeper into her mouth. His legs stiffened beneath her. He moaned and urged her to pull back. She denied this request. The taste of his essence was as sweet as her love for him.

When the pulsating of his manhood subsided, she finally backed away, and once again left the bed. She did not turn off the lights after she'd procured a condom. Demon's manhood continued to throb with anticipation as she applied it before mounting him. She almost climaxed while sliding her hot moistness down onto him. But Demon's broad chest shuddered, and he reached for her breasts, and she was determined to continue pleasing him until he was fully satiated.

CHAPTER FIVE
UPPITY NIGGERS

That night, Demon and Zahra appreciated the luxury of sleeping for a solid nine hours. The next morning, they indulged in a leisurely breakfast with several of their comrades, before Cujo arrived at the headquarters at 10 am. While most members of Ace of Spades lived a transient lifestyle and had separated from their families for safety reasons, Cujo was married with two children. He never spent the night at their headquarters. And like the computer guys, he provided operational support, rather than get involved with the group's bloody work.

He entered the kitchen and greeted the team before locking eyes with Demon.

Demon rose from the table and took one more sip of his coffee before asking, "You ready to have our talk?"

Cujo nodded. "I don't think anyone's in that bedroom down the hall."

"Alright," Demon said. "I'm right behind you."

When they were alone in the room, Cujo closed the door. The bedroom was sparsely furnished. Other than a bed and nightstand, there was only a small desk with one chair. Cujo stepped past the chair. Demon was about to have a seat there, but Cujo didn't sit on the bed, so Demon remained standing as well.

The men watched each other for a moment before Demon asked, "What's been up with you?"

Cujo shrugged. "Nothing much. Same old, same old."

"How's the family?"

"Everybody good."

Demon nodded. "That's good to hear. Listen, I'm pretty sure I know why you scheduled the meeting. For the sake of transparency, I want you to know that I talked to Tasha and Zulu last night. They said you don't like that we killed that boy. You wanna start there?"

"You feel differently?" Cujo asked. "You think that was a good idea?"

"Well, yeah. I do." Before the taller man asked why, Demon offered the same rationale he'd been using. "The boy was a witness, plus I'm pretty sure he would've grown up hating niggas just like his dad. He would'a been a mass shooting waiting to happen if we let him live. Now he's a hashtag. I like that better."

Cujo shook his head. "Seems like you getting more coldhearted by the day."

"I don't see how you can look at the same news as me and *not* start to feel like this. The one last month, how many was it – five or six of our people killed?"

"You talking about in El Paso? Those were *Mexicans*. You counting them as *our people* now?"

Demon nodded. "Anybody who get killed because they happen to have a certain skin color are my people. Any white man doing the shooting 'cause they think they're being replaced in this country is my enemy. That's always been the case."

"Since you keep your eyes on the news so much, how do you feel about what they're saying about your video?" Cujo wondered.

"*My* video?" Demon chuckled at that. "You putting the whole operation in my lap? Don't forget it was your idea to go after the militia in the first place."

"I know that was my idea. Didn't say it wasn't."

"Okay. I'm just checking, because it seems like you trying to change your tune after the fact."

"It wasn't my idea to make that video. I didn't know nothing about it till after it got released. You gon' tell me I'm wrong about that?"

"No, the video was my idea. But you *did* know about stringing 'em up. You were okay with that."

Shaking his head, Cujo said, "No, I wasn't."

"Okay, now this is that shit I'm talking about. You know we talked about hanging them from the trees. We had that conversation face-to-face."

"I agreed with you doing it because you said the mission wasn't happening unless you got to add your little touch to it. *That's* what happened. I gave you a concession, and like always, you took it way too far."

"Let me get this straight. You were okay with us hanging them, but you don't like that I recorded it...? Can you tell me how the recording changes anything? Don't you think *somebody* was gon' take a picture once they found those bodies, and at some point, people was gon' see the picture?"

"No. Not necessarily. Crime scene photos don't always get leaked."

"Well, I see it the other way," Demon said. "Even if the pictures didn't get leaked, the police would've reported on how they found the bodies. Everybody was gon' know one way or another. I figured I might as well put my little artistic spin on it, so we could control the narrative."

Cujo's nostrils flared as he sighed. "You proud of that video, aren't you?"

"It's some of my finest work," Demon said nodding.

"And you think everybody in the group is cool with it? What about Einstein? I know he helped you make it. Do you think he wanted to do that?"

Demon realized he'd spoken to Tasha and Zulu last night but failed to include the computer guys in his little meeting. He should've known Cujo had gotten to Einstein first, and possibly tainted his opinion.

He said, "I think Einstein was cool with it."

"That's the problem with you. You never ask anyone how they feel. You just give orders, and people obey. You do what's right for *you*, never taking the rest of our opinions into consideration. I guess you not worried about what they saying about us on the news…"

"Cujo, we been killing people for years. Most of 'em because we thought they were about to do something they hadn't actually done yet. They been vilifying us on the news ever since we started leaving our calling card."

"Another one of your brilliant ideas…"

"Yes, another one of my ideas *that we voted on*. You gave your reasons for not wanting to leave the card, and I gave mine. My side won – by a two-thirds majority. You need to move on."

"Two-thirds ain't one hundred percent," Cujo countered. "Two-thirds means a third of our group never wanted to take credit for those killings. And I'm betting even more than that don't like the idea of you posting that video. What you're doing is making us look like *monsters* – worse than the people we going after."

"We're *revolutionaries*," Demon said, barely able to hide his irritation. "We can't avenge our martyrs with weakness."

"You think I'm weak because I don't wanna kill kids or make videos taunting our enemies?"

"No, but I think our enemies got no problem doing either of those things. The last one went live on

Facebook, made sure to wear a harness for his cellphone on his chest, so both hands would be free for his assault rifle. He killed whatever black face he saw in that store – old people, young people, *whoever* – as long as they were black. It's okay for them to do that, but if I do something similar, I'm a monster?"

Cujo couldn't help but tell him, "You named yourself *Demon*. I think that says a lot."

Demon took the jab in stride. "Yeah. It does. When they see me coming, they should know they about to go to hell."

"I see I ain't getting nowhere with you. That's why I called the meeting."

"And what exactly do you plan to say at this meeting?" Demon wondered. "You wanna get another vote on something that already happened? You wanna vote on whether I should be *censored*? Don't you ever get tired of trying to divide this group? Me and you, we supposed to be a united front."

"How can we be united," Cujo wondered, "if you constantly doing shit I don't agree with?"

"Look, I'ma ask you again," Demon said, sneering now, "what is this meeting for? If you think I'ma stand in front of our people and argue with you like we doing now, you might as well cancel it. We need to be united now, more than ever."

"You want me to *lie* and say I agree with what you did? I'm not doing that."

"Well, one of us is gon' have to say something."

"Since you so good at defending yourself, how about you do all the talking?" Cujo offered. "Tell 'em why you did what you did, and let them decide if they down with you or not."

Demon was surprised that Cujo would suggest such a thing. He quickly seized on it, before he could change his mind. "That's the best idea you had in a long time. I'm all for that. Thank you."

Flustered, Cujo said, "Are you gonna ask them how they feel about it, or just talk at them?"

"I promise I'll ask them how they feel," Demon said. "I'll give them an opportunity to tell me if they not down with it. Is that it? We cool?"

Cujo shook his head. "I think I'll wait to see how the meeting goes, before I respond to that."

Demon shrugged. "Whatever, man." He turned and left the room.

∞ ∞ ∞ ∞ ∞ ∞ ∞

By noon, a majority of the group had arrived for the one o'clock meeting. At that point, their total membership was 52. The living room, kitchen, and adjacent dining room could accommodate them all, but few were lucky enough to find a chair or a stool. Cujo didn't always make the best decisions, but he had instructed the group to take Ubers to this location, rather than line the block and adjacent blocks with their cars.

Demon had a few hours to prepare for the meeting, but he wasn't one for scripted speeches. He preferred to speak from the heart. If things didn't go his way, he'd apologize and inform them that going forward, Cujo would have the final say in what occurred during their missions. The good thing was, Demon was cool with the group's response either way. As long as he still had the opportunity to kill white folks who hated black folks, he'd consider it a win.

With this mind state, he was as cool as ever when all but three members of the group had arrived at the headquarters, and he commenced the meeting at 1 pm sharp.

Looking out at the crowd, eighty percent of whom he'd recruited personally, he first thanked them for adjusting their schedules so they could be in attendance.

He then said, "Let me ask y'all something. Y'all know what an *uppity nigger* is?"

The question drew the confusion he'd expected. He grinned at the stunned faces staring at him.

"They don't use that term anymore," he said. "But that's what they used to call us – not all of us. But some of our ancestors had the honor of being called an *uppity nigger*. Back in the day," he explained, "you could become an uppity nigger for a lot of reasons. I'm talking *way* back, in the days of slavery and Jim Crow. You could be called an uppity nigger for learning to read. You could be an uppity nigger for saying your name ain't Toby, it's *Kunta Kinte*.

"They called us uppity if we refused to sit at the back of the bus, or if we tried to organize a boycott against segregated bathrooms. Uppity niggers went against the status quo. They said, '*Fuck you, whitey. I am a man, and you will treat me as such.*' Yeah," he said with a grin. "We come from a long line of uppity niggers. I ain't never read this nowhere, so I'm prolly the first one to say it out loud, but Obama may have been the most uppitiest uppity nigger we done ever had. That man said fuck the status quo all the way to the White House. It don't get more gangsta than that."

Most of the crowd was either smiling or chuckling now. What he was saying wasn't a con, but Demon knew he had them. He didn't have to imagine what was going through Cujo's mind at that moment. The second leader of the group stood right beside him. Demon didn't look over to see his reaction.

His tone became somber as he continued. "Emmett Till was uppity. He said, '*Fuck these rules y'all got in the south. I can talk to whoever I want.*' Medgar Evers, yeah, he was uppity. Martin Luther King Jr., Malcom X, Fred Hampton – our enemies hated those uppity niggers so much they had to take 'em out. They had to, because uppity niggers turn *regular* niggas into uppity niggers, and that's something they just can't stand. Could you imagine a whole country full of uppity niggas? Could you imagine a group, only *fifty-two* strong, filled with uppity niggas who ain't got no problem killing a racist white man? Can you imagine the damage they could do to the status quo? If you can't, look around at the people standing next to you. That's what it looks like. I know I'm uppity, and since that's something white folks can't stand, I'ma embrace the term. But we at a crossroads right now, so y'all gon' have to do some soul-searching to decide if you wanna embrace it too."

After a moment, he said, "We're here today because of what happened in North Dakota. Most of you were involved with those missions. It's been brought to my attention that some of you don't agree with certain things that transpired. Specifically, I'm talking about the teenager who was killed and what we did to the bodies in the woods. As for the boy, I gave the okay to kill him. He was a witness, and we never leave witnesses behind. If he was completely innocent, I may have made an exception. But that boy was armed. He pulled a gun on one of our brothers. He had to die."

Demon waited a few beats before saying, "As far as the lynchings, that was my call too. I wanted to do that, so I could create the video you've all seen by now. I know we're getting a lot of backlash because of that video. It may be uncomfortable to read some of that stuff. But the thing is, they're saying exactly what I want them to say. I want the world to be mad at us and scared of us. We are not Boy Scouts. The media has always felt that what we're doing is wrong. That video changes nothing. That video is for our enemies. It's a small piece of atonement for the lynchings they did to our people. If you Google *lynching*, you can see plenty of pictures of what they did to us, but you would never see that we got revenge on them. That changed yesterday."

Demon surveyed the room. Everyone was watching him closely. No one spoke.

"I've been told that I went too far," he continued. "I've been told that some of you no longer want to be associated with a group that will put out a video like that. I don't regret any part of our mission, but I want to apologize for not including you in some of the bigger decisions I made. I was wrong for that."

Demon paused again, hoping the sincerity of his apology would resonate.

"Anyway, I wanna do something I ain't never done before. Right now, I'm giving any of you who want to leave the group an open invitation to do so. If you don't like the direction we're going – the direction I'm taking us – you can opt out. No hard feelings. If you walk out right now, we will no longer contact you, and I'll make sure you get half of your retirement package."

He waited. No one moved.

Demon sighed before saying, "Okay, I'd like to think no one is leaving because you all want to remain in this group. But I know it's probably some herd mentality going on. Some of you want to leave, but you don't want people looking at you funny if you walk out. That's understandable. I'll give you another option: After this meeting, you can text me. It'll be private.

Just say, 'I'm out,' and everything I said still goes. We won't contact you again, outside of giving you half of your retirement. Is that cool?"

A few faces in the crowd looked around. Some nodded. Demon wasn't sure if the nods meant they would text him later and exit the group discreetly. Time would tell. He looked over at Cujo. The bigger man kept a straight face, but Demon could tell he was seething.

"Alright," he said. "I guess that's that. For those of you who choose to remain in the group but also feel some kind of way about my video, I want you to do me a favor. Actually, I want you to do this for yourself. I want you to do some research on the Red Summer of 1919. There was racial violence in over 25 cities across the country. This all culminated with the Tulsa massacre in 1921. I want you to learn about what they did to us, and how we didn't do anything to deserve it. I could tell you what happened, but I think it's better if you learn things on your own. We're all revolutionaries, but we're also historians. After researching that, ask yourself if my video makes a little more sense..."

More faces in the crowd nodded. A few people reached for their phone and started typing. Demon couldn't have been more pleased with the way things were going.

"Since transparency is something I know I struggle with," he continued, "I wanna let y'all know how things will go moving forward. Starting today, we're embarking on an expansion mission. This will include more tactical points and more new recruits. Usually, I do most of the recruiting. That's gon' change. We currently have 52 members. I wanna double that within six months. To pull this off, I'm gon' train some of y'all on how to vet people. These background checks are more important now than ever, because the danger of being infiltrated is real. The feds are trying their best to find out who we are, and they're very good at what they do.

"Speaking of safety, all of you who are still holding on to your regular lives need to be extra careful. Head and Einstein are on top of things, when it comes to external threats. But we all have to be vigilant. We need to have that *gangbanger* mentality. You know what I mean. I'm talking about the guy in the hood who's been shot a couple of times, and he's always looking over his shoulder, because he knows his opps are still out there, gunning for him. We need to have that kind of mind state. Our threats could be the police or other militias who want to get revenge for what happened in North Dakota. Your safety is my number one priority."

Demon paused again, to let that sink in.

"The last thing I want to do in this meeting," he said, "is give y'all an opportunity to speak. I know y'all got some questions, and it'll be a while before we're all gathered together like this. I want y'all to speak freely.

You can ask me anything or say whatever you want. The floor is open..."

The Q & A portion of the meeting lasted thirty minutes. After Bubba broke the ice by asking, "Have we reached the point to where we might need to start looking into security?" the rest of the group was comfortable enough to express their concerns, opinions, and ask other questions. Demon responded to most of these. He deferred to the computer guys when the answers were out of his realm of expertise. And despite his opposition to Demon getting his way –*again* – Cujo stepped up to the plate and participated in the conversation.

By the time all questions had been fielded, Demon was fairly confident no member of the group would choose to depart. When not speaking, he checked his phone intermittently. So far, he had not received any text messages.

When the meeting officially concluded, he announced, "I know it's pretty crowded in here, and some of y'all have places to be, but I got some food coming from one of my favorite soul food joints. I would like it if y'all stick around and get something to eat, before you hit the road."

Most of the group took him up on the offer.

∞ ∞ ∞ ∞ ∞ ∞ ∞

An hour later, the house was filled with good-cooking, lighthearted conversations and laughter. Zahra had been trying to get close to her man, but she had to wait a while, until there was a break in the line of people who wanted to speak to Demon personally. When her time finally came, she sidled up to him.

"*Mr. Popular*, as always," she teased.

"Nah, they just needed reassurances," he said, grinning. "How do you think it went?"

"Your speech?"

"Yeah, the whole meeting."

"Your speech was awesome. I always thought being an uppity nigger was a bad thing. Now I wanna put it on a tee shirt."

He chuckled. "Don't go doing that any time soon. A bunch of folks out there looking for our uppity asses."

She nodded. Smiling. "I'm proud of you."

His brow furrowed. "For what? I didn't do nothing special."

"I think that's one of the most special things about you – that you don't know how special you are."

He considered that before saying. "Thanks. I appreciate that." He switched gears and asked, "From your vantage point, how was Cujo reacting? I wanted to look over at him a few times, but if he had that stank face on, I didn't want to draw attention to it."

"He was cool," she said. "I saw his lips tighten every now and then, like he wanted to jump in and say something. But I don't think anyone else caught it. I only noticed because I was watching him, probably as much as I was watching you."

"What you think gon' happen with him?" Demon wondered.

"As far as..."

"As far as moving forward."

"Maybe he'll send you a text message saying he's out," Zahra joked.

"Shit, if I could only be that lucky."

"Is that what you want?" she asked seriously.

He shrugged. "I don't know. He does a lot of good things for the group. And he's a founding father. But it's frustrating, the way he's always coming at me."

"Maybe that's what you need," she said, smiling again, "someone to keep you in check. If you got to do everything your way, you'd prolly have Head and Einstein trying to build a nuke in the backyard."

Demon laughed. Zahra loved to see that, his smile, the twinkle in his eyes when he was amused.

He told her, "I volunteered you for the recruitment drive, by the way."

"Oh yeah?"

He nodded. "It's about time you got good at something else, other than killing."

"Okay. You gon' train me?"

"Of course."

"Let me ask you something: Before the meeting, did you talk to Cujo about your plan to double the group's membership?"

He shook his head. "Nope."

That cracked her up. "Just admit it. You *trying* to run him off."

Demon continued to smile but didn't respond to that.

CHAPTER SIX
CHARLEY'S

By ten o'clock things had died down at the Houston headquarters, and most of the group had dispersed to destinations across the country.

There was always much work to do.

The brains of the operation met in the computer room to strategize their next moves. This core group consisted of Demon, Cujo, Head and Einstein. All four men were seated, the computer guys in their office chairs, Demon on a futon and Cujo in a chair on the opposite side of the room. Cujo surprised Demon by kicking off the brainstorming session with a compliment.

"You did good today. You always know what to say, when to say it, and how to say it."

"Thanks," Demon replied. "To be honest, I didn't really plan for that meeting. Wasn't sure what I was gon' say till people started showing up."

"I've seen the way you captivate a crowd, quite a few times," Cujo said. "That's a skill not too many of our leaders possess. Listening to you today, I was reminded of Fred Hampton. The way you establish the buy-in. That's a skill I don't have. That's one of the reasons why you're so important to this group."

Demon was taken aback. It had been a long time since Cujo had spoken so candidly and highly of him. He didn't know if this meant Cujo was willing to put their differences behind them, but Demon was eager to take the high road as well.

"Do y'all remember how we started?" he reminisced. "In the beginning, we were working out of a hotel. Just the four of us, a few laptops and a few pistols. Now look at us. Look how far we've come. You mentioned Fred Hampton. I know I'm not on that level, but that's how groups like the Panthers started. A few revolutionaries with an idea that turned into an agenda, and then it turned into a movement." He looked each man in the eye one by one and nodded. "I think it's good to look back on our humble beginnings every now and then. I know things ain't always perfect, but the more people we get, the better we get."

"That's why you wanna kick off a recruitment drive," Cujo stated.

Demon nodded. "Sorry I didn't mention that before the meeting. I would'a told you, but like I said, things started coming to me at the last minute. I think it was when I saw all of those people here today that I thought, '*Damn. What if we had twice as many, or three times more soldiers?*"

"On that point," Head said, swiveling his chair towards his desktop, "I think you'll be happy to know that our candidate pool is skyrocketing. We usually see a lil bump in these numbers after our missions, but it's never been like this. Your video lit a fire under some people. I've already found over 300 possible recruits. Granted, a good number of them might be federal agents, but still." He pulled up a spreadsheet he'd been working on, where he was collecting information on these individuals.

"What do you look for when you find these recruits?" Cujo asked. "I know the process is a lot different than when I used to do it..."

"Social media brings in the most candidates," Head informed him. "I know there's a lot of people online talking about how much they hate us, but it's damn near as many who say they support us. Me and Einstein built a program to scrutinize all of those tweets and Facebook posts. We start broad, looking for people who support the killings or mention Ace of Spades directly and have positive things to say. The same system starts tracking certain people, looking at their past tweets. This is where we start to find red flags."

"Like what?" Cujo asked.

"Like how long their account's been active," Einstein jumped in. "New accounts that start posting about how they wanna join the Ace of Spades is usually a cop. I know there are some people out there who create a Twitter account because they saw something on the news and want to start a dialogue, but I don't trust them. If one of our supporters has an old account, we wanna know if they been supporting black causes for a while. One of the dudes we weeded out this morning didn't bother to scrub his old tweets before he tried to infiltrate us. He been a right-wing, Trump-loving fanatic for years. But now, all of a sudden he starts talking about how he's down with what we're doing, and he wishes we had a website, so he could get in touch with us about joining our group."

"That dude was an idiot," Head said. "Or maybe they're just underestimating us. Either way, we're more prepared for their trickery than they think we are. Most of the people on this list are solid," he said, referencing his spreadsheet. "They sound like Tasha did, when we decided to recruit her. But that doesn't mean we can bring them all in. They still have to be vetted."

"It takes a special kind of person to go from hating racists," Demon chimed in, "to being willing to pick up a gun and actually do something about it."

"What's the likelihood that some of the people on that list will lead to us getting infiltrated?" Cujo wanted to know.

"There's always a chance," Head said. "That's where Demon comes in. He's the best at vetting people. Has never let a bad apple slip through."

"No, I think y'all are the ones who deserve the credit," Demon said. "Y'all do all the heavy lifting. By the time the list gets to me, I'm just looking for people with a killer instinct. Y'all never told me to follow up on somebody who turned out to be a cop."

"You said you wanted to train some of our people to start vetting," Cujo recalled. "What if they not as good as you? What if they fuck up, and the feds make it all the way to our headquarters?"

"Everything we do is risky," Demon stated. "Every mission, every group meeting. There are always risks. The ends justify the means."

"I'm not saying you wrong about wanting more soldiers," Cujo replied. "But help me understand; what's wrong with the 52 we got right now? I think we been doing a good job. Don't you think that if we stick with these people who have already proven themselves, we can cut out some of these risks you're willing to take?"

"Of course we would," Demon agreed. "But we can't hit the number of killings I want if our group remains small. After what we pulled off in North Dakota, I been thinking that if we had more people, we can try to flood the system."

Cujo frowned. *Flood the system?*

"*With bodies,*" Demon said. "Think about how many detectives we put to work in North Dakota. I mean, yeah, that increases our risks. A lot more people trying to find us. But what if we did coordinated attacks like that across the country, all on the same day? A hundred people committing a hundred murders on the same day, all leaving our calling card. What if we did something like that three days in a row? I know the FBI got thousands of special agents, but that many crime scenes gon' be hard to investigate after a while. The busier they are, the harder it'll be for them to stay focused."

"That's ambitious," Cujo said.

"Better than that, it's *possible*," Demon stated. "Just gotta get our numbers up. Do you think you might wanna get in on this recruiting? You used to be real good at it."

"Actually, I think I'll stick to setting up the tactical points," Cujo decided. "You said we need more of those, right? We'll need more headquarters, more vehicles. I'd rather work on behind the scenes stuff like that. If one of these new recruits turns out to be an undercover, I don't want to be responsible for letting them in."

Ol' scary ass nigga.

Demon caught himself before saying that aloud.

Instead, he told Cujo, "That's cool. That's important work too."

∞ ∞ ∞ ∞ ∞ ∞ ∞

Two days later, on a Wednesday afternoon, Demon was with his favorite trainee in the sunshine state. More specifically, they sat in the parking lot of an

Olive Garden restaurant on North Westshore Drive, not far from Tampa International Airport. Across the street from them was another restaurant, Ocean Prime. It was there that Zahra planned to meet her first, personally vetted new recruit.

While she enjoyed the murder aspect of her job immensely, there was something about the recruitment process that was equally exhilarating. This was partly because of her recollection of how she felt when Demon first made contact with her. That was almost two years ago, at her grandmother's funeral. Her granny, along with 17 more black souls, was gunned down at a neighborhood Walmart by a white supremacist. After the gravesite service, Demon had approached her and said he understood how she felt, and she wasn't wrong to feel that way. She would never forget his boldness, the way he looked her in the eyes and seemed to read her mind.

My name's David. But my friends call me Demon. Can I give you my number? I want you to call me when you feel like you might wanna take action yourself, instead of waiting for someone to solve our problems.

Given the whirlwind of emotions she was experiencing at the time, it was hard to focus on how she would go on living without her grandmother, let alone figure out what the dark stranger meant by *take action yourself.*

Zahra was now in a position to offer the same proposal to another tormented brother who did not know that he had the power to become a revolutionary and a soldier.

Another thing Zahra enjoyed about recruiting was the cat-and-mouse game of trying to figure out if the recruit was really who they said they were.

Demon had warned her, "If you pick the wrong one, you'll be lucky if it's actually a cop. The worst they can do is arrest you. If it's one of our real enemies, they might pull out a gun and blow your brains out right then and there. You gotta be 100 percent positive about the person you're talking to before you even *think* about a face-to-face."

The next step, after meeting the recruit, would be to determine if they were willing to take up arms against their enemies. Not until the candidate had blood on their hands, would they be admitted into the Ace of Spades.

In the restaurant parking lot, Zahra and Demon did not appear furtive. From all outward appearances, they were either a couple who had just arrived for a late afternoon meal, or maybe they had recently dined and longed for a few more moments in each other's presence, before they left the restaurant in separate vehicles. Either way, there was nothing to see here.

They had parked facing Westshore, which gave them an excellent view of the other restaurant across the street. Because this was her first time, Demon had asked Zahra to conduct all of her communications with the candidate on speaker, while he listened. In the past eight days leading up to this encounter, she'd communicated with a man named John Gilliam several times. John was shocked the first time she called him. He asked all the pertinent questions, wanting to know who she was and how she got his number. She had been as elusive with him as Demon was when they first met.

She had told him, "I'll explain more about myself later. What I need to know is if I'm contacting the right person. I know you've been talking about how upset you are about the things that's been going on in this country, as far as the mass murders against black people. I wanna meet with you, to talk about finding a way to do something about it."

He immediately asked her, "Are you a cop? Is this some kind of set up?"

Zahra remembered grinning as she shook her head. She'd told him, "I'm a lot of bad things, John, but I promise you a cop ain't one of 'em..."

After watching the Ocean Prime parking lot for several minutes, Zahra asked Demon, who was in the driver's seat, "Is there something I should be looking for?"

"You tell me," he said. "You're about to call John and tell him to meet you there. What do you think you should be looking for?"

While training her, Demon responded to most of Zahra's questions with more questions. She no longer found this irritating.

"Checking to make sure there are no police in the area?" she offered.

He nodded. "Yeah, for sure. Is that it?"

She shrugged. "I don't know. Tell me."

"After you call him, you wanna make sure he comes alone."

She pursed her lips. She knew that.

"What kind of car does he drive?" Demon asked.

"A black Honda Accord." She gave him the license plate number.

"Where's his driver's license?"

She pulled up the image on her phone.

"So you know what he drives, and you know what he looks like," Demon said. "You shouldn't have any trouble spotting him when he shows up. Always let him go in first and wait on you. If everything looks legit, then you go and have your talk with him. That's when you'll be the most vulnerable. I won't be in there with you."

"You want me to call you and put you on speaker before I go in, right?"

"Yeah, but if he makes a move while you're in there, I might not be fast enough to stop it. You gotta be prepared to defend yourself."

"I am." Zahra reached subconsciously for the purse in her lap. Inside it was a snub nose .44 special. That bad boy could drop a bear.

"I know you got that, but you gotta be *prepared* to defend yourself," he stressed. "For you, that may look like a hand in yo purse under the table. You get me?"

Zahra nodded. "You know I can defend myself."

Demon did know that, but he remained apprehensive. "Alright," he said. "Go ahead and call him."

Zahra placed the call. On speaker, they listened to the man answer.

"Hey, Nessa? Are we still meeting today? I'm ready."

"Yes," she told him. "There's a restaurant not too far from you. *Ocean Prime.* Do you know where that is?"

"Yeah, on Westshore?"

"That's the one. How long will it take for you to get there?"

"Not long. About fifteen minutes."

"Come alone," Zahra instructed him. "Go inside and get a table for two. Tell the lady up front what your name is and let her know you're expecting a date. I'll come to your table when I get there."

"Okay. Thanks for meeting me. I'm excited to hear what you have to say."

"Alright. I'll see you in a few," Zahra said and disconnected. She wasn't sure why she felt as nervous as she did. She blew out a sigh and looked over at Demon. "Did I do good?"

He nodded. "That was perfect."

They waited.

Twelve minutes later, they saw John's car enter the parking lot. He found a spot not far from the entrance and exited the vehicle. He was alone. He looked around, not too much, before disappearing inside. Demon continued to survey the scene like a hawk.

They waited.

When five more minutes passed, Zahra asked, "Is it time for me to go? I don't see anything wrong."

Demon looked through his phone, rather than respond. He then instructed her to, "Call him back and tell him you want to meet somewhere else. Don't give him a reason. Tell him to meet you at..." He checked the information he'd found on his phone. "Charley's Steak House. It's around the corner, on West Cypress, less than a mile away."

"Okay," Zahra said, her heart starting to drum uncomfortably. "Is something wrong? Did I miss something?"

"I don't know yet," Demon said, his eyes back on the parking lot. "Make the call, and I'll know for sure."

She wished he would tell her what he was thinking, but she understood that wasn't always his way. Despite their bond, he continued to keep his cards close to his chest at times. She called the recruit again.

"Hi," John answered. "Are you here? I got us a table. Actually, it's a booth. Is that okay?"

"Change of plans," Zahra said. "Meet me at Charley's Steak House. It's around the corner, on Cypress – *West Cypress*. It's less than a mile away. When you get there, do the same as you did at Ocean Prime."

"Okay. Is something wrong?"

"No. Nothing's wrong. Plans change sometimes. It's no big deal."

"Okay," John said. "I'll head over there now."

While they waited for him to leave the restaurant, Zahra watched the parking lot, more keenly than before. One vehicle exited and one entered before John made it to his car. He left the restaurant and headed to the other restaurant.

Demon sighed, shaking his head. He told her, "I'm not gon' play the guessing game with you this time. I do want to know if you saw what I saw, though. If not, I'll tell you why I told you to call him back."

Zahra felt like a complete failure. She told him, "No. I didn't see anything."

"Before John got there," Demon explained, "a gray Tahoe got there before him. Did you see it?"

"I – I think so."

"After we told him to go to the other restaurant," Demon continued, "the Tahoe left, heading in the direction of the steak house. But nobody ever got out of the Tahoe while it was at Ocean Prime. What are the odds that the people in the Tahoe had the same change of plans as John?"

Zahra's eyes widened. She swallowed what felt like a dry nickel in her throat.

"I think you're being set up," Demon said. "We won't know for sure until we get to the steak house. If the Tahoe is there, then the gig is up; John is communicating with whoever is in that SUV. But before we go to Charley's, we gotta do our research."

He lifted his phone and placed a call.

"Hey... Yeah, what's up, man... Hey, listen, I need you to check something for me. Run the plate for a gray 2021 Tahoe." He gave the person on the other end of the line the license plate.

Zahra knew he was talking to either Head or Einstein. She was amazed that not only had Demon spotted the suspicious vehicle, but he managed to memorize the license plate. Compared to him, she was an amateur. She felt like she didn't deserve the time he was investing in her.

Demon listened to whichever computer guy he was talking to, and said, "Okay... Uh huh... Yeah..." and then, "Call me back when you get that." He disconnected and looked at his woman.

To Zahra, he said, "The person driving the Tahoe is a white man named William Pearse. Head's gonna dig deeper and see what the internet got on him. I'm not trying to make you feel bad, but did you notice if

William had an occupant with him in the Tahoe? It's okay if you don't know."

Zahra shook her head. She wasn't a weak woman, but she was on the verge of tears.

"He did," Demon said. "But it's okay that you didn't catch that." He reached over and rubbed her leg comfortingly. He started the car and backed out of the parking spot. "Let's go see if the Tahoe is at Charley's waiting on you."

They didn't pull into the parking lot at the steakhouse. They didn't have to. From the street, they spotted John's Honda and William's Tahoe at the location. Demon drove right on by.

"Where we going?" Zahra asked. "What happens now?"

"We're going back to the hotel," Demon said. "What happens now depends on—"

His phone rang.

"What happens now depends on what Head has to say," Demon said as he answered the call. This time the car's Bluetooth picked it up, and Zahra was able to listen to both sides of the conversation.

"So, that William fellow is a member of the Proud Boys," Head informed them. "He hasn't been talking too reckless on the internet, but you know how that group is. The feds are on their ass because of that January 6th shit, among other things. Aren't you in Florida? I thought you and Cleo were looking into a new recruit..."

"We are. William is showing up at all the meeting spots we arrange with the recruit," Demon informed him. "Since William gets there first, I got no choice but to believe John is tipping him off. To confirm that, could you look into John Gilliam's phone records and see if he called or texted William in the past thirty minutes. No need to rush on that. Me and Cleo are headed back to the hotel."

"Alright. Gotcha," Head said. "Sorry about that. I thought John was solid."

"Not your fault. You did your job. That's why you got us to do this other part. 'Preciate you. Holler at you later." He disconnected.

As they continued to the hotel, Zahra asked him, "What tipped you off? I wanna think like you, but it's hard."

"To be honest," Demon said, "I don't know if I would've caught that if not for you. I never want to put you in harm's way, so I was extra careful. I was suspicious when I saw the guys sitting in the Tahoe. They got there right before John, but they didn't go inside. That's why it's important to get there early. We was watching when the Tahoe pulled in, and we saw John come in after them. John went inside, and we made him wait for five minutes. During that time, the people in the Tahoe just sat there. And then, of course, when we told John to go to Charley's, all of a sudden the Tahoe got moving."

Zahra took a deep breath. "But, but why would John be connected to the Proud Boys? I been through all of his social media. He seemed like he was against those kinds of groups. What did I miss?"

"That's a mystery," Demon acknowledged. "Maybe he ran his mouth after you contacted him. Maybe he told some of his white friends, and they told some of their white friends, and one thing led to another. Next thing you know, William gets in contact with John and tells him he'll give him $10,000 if he gives him the location of the meeting. John don't know you, don't know what you plan to tell him, but somebody wants to pay him for something he was gonna do already – why not take it?

"But, like I said, I don't know if that's what happened. The phone records will probably show that John called somebody *other* than William. That may have been the passenger in the Tahoe. If we find out who *that* person is, we'll see how he's connected to William. It would take a while to put those pieces together, but in the end, we may never know how this happened – unless we have a sit down with John and make him tell us why he did what he did. Am I gonna do all of that? Naw. I care, but at the same time, I don't care *that* much. I got you out of harm's way, and that's what I care about.

"One thing I am gon' do is put William *and* John at the top of my to-do list. I don't know what these sneaky motherfuckers got going on, but it just cost both of 'em their lives. You got a problem with that?"

Zahra shook her head. "No, but I feel like I failed you. David, I don't know if I should be recruiting people. This, this might be too much for me."

He surprised her by smiling. "You sound like every kid that done ever fell off a bike. I feel a little weird telling you this, but if you give up every time something doesn't go your way the first time, you'll never get anywhere in life."

She smiled back at him. "Why you feel weird telling me that?"

"Because that's something I imagined myself telling my son one day, not my woman."

She nodded. She took another deep breath. When she blew it out this time, she felt a lot better.

"Sometimes adults need to be reminded of that too. I learned a lot today. I promise I won't let something like this happen again."

"I know you won't. Hey, since we got some time on our hands, you wanna get something to eat? I'm in the mood for steak."

She laughed. "Oh, you got jokes."

"No, I'm serious. You ain't hungry?"

"Yes, and I wouldn't mind a steak – anywhere but *Charley's*."

"For sure," he said. "Anywhere but there."

CHAPTER SEVEN
THE SILENT MINORITY

The couple didn't enjoy much downtime in the Sunshine State before hopping on another plane. They touched down in Des Moines, Iowa after the two-and-a-half-hour flight. They first headed to a public storage facility in the Linden Heights District. Here, they swapped their rental for two vehicles that had been stashed there. Demon took dibs on the Charger. Zahra slid behind the wheel of a Camry. She would've preferred something with a little more muscle under the hood, but the TRD was Camry's fastest model. If she wasn't able to book it to safety in this car, a few more horses under the hood probably wouldn't help. Both cars had duffle bags in their trunks. They didn't have to check to know that these bags contained all of the firepower they needed.

From the storage unit, they headed to a tactical point in Laurel Hill. There, they planned to meet up with two more soldiers who would assist with the missions in the area. Both of these operatives were female. Zahra planned to work with Simone. Demon's partner in crime was Jewell. Neither of these ladies had arrived at the tactical point when they pulled in. Demon didn't stay long before preparing to hit the road again. He wanted to get started on surveilling his target.

Before he took off, Zahra asked him, "Can you tell me again why we're not working together? Whose idea was it for us to work with other people?"

He grinned at her. "What's wrong with working with other people?"

"Nothing's wrong with it. I'm just wondering why you split us up."

"A couple of reasons," Demon said. "For one, Jewell is new to the group. I haven't had much contact with her since I recruited her. She's smart, but I think she needs more training on the subtleties of our operations."

"You feel like this training needs to come directly from you?"

Still smiling, he said, "Not necessarily. But since I'm here, I think it's the best course of action. What's the problem? You don't like the idea of me training another woman?"

Zahra hoped that wasn't what she was feeling. When she first joined the group, Demon was single. Despite her attraction to him, his interactions with her were always professional. If she had not seduced him one night (might as well call it what it was), they probably would've maintained their platonic relationship.

"No, I don't have a problem with it," she decided. "What's the other reason?"

"Huh? Oh, I think it's good to work with others so they can get to know us more, and we can get to know them. The bigger our group gets, the more we can start to feel like a crowd of strangers."

She nodded. "I get that." She stepped to him and gave him a hug before he headed for the garage. "Happy hunting."

"Same to you. What time are y'all taking off?"

"Not sure. I'll strategize with Simone when she gets here."

"If I'm not back before you leave, tell Jewell to call me, and I'll come pick her up."

"Okay, I will."

∞ ∞ ∞ ∞ ∞ ∞ ∞

A few hours later, night had fallen, and the bustle of the busy city had mostly died down on what had thus far been a mundane Monday. Zahra and Simone sat in the parking lot of a McDonalds in Lower Beaver. Inside the restaurant, they had eyes on their target, who was dining with his daughter. Zahra guessed the girl's age to be around thirteen. Upon seeing the girl, Zahra's thoughts returned to the teenager Tasha and Zulu decided to kill in North Dakota. Apparently, Simone was thinking the same.

Without looking away from the restaurant's glass windows, she said, "I don't care what position that baby put us in, I ain't killing no little girl..."

Simone had rich, dark skin. She wore her hair short and curly. She had small eyes and full lips. She was approximately Zahra's height and build. A prominent gap between her top front teeth did not detract from her beauty.

"I don't wanna kill that girl, either," Zahra replied. "Shouldn't be no reason why we'd have to."

"You not wanting to kill her ain't the same as me saying I'm *not gonna* kill her," Simone said, looking over at her. "You don't like giving assurances, or you been sipping that Kool-Aid?"

Lines of confusion appeared on Zahra's forehead. *"Sipping that Kool-Aid?"*

"The one Demon serving y'all. Seem like he got everybody wrapped around his finger. I'm down for the cause as much as anybody else. But I'm a thinker, too. I don't need nobody doing my thinking for me."

Startled, it occurred to Zahra that Simone did not know that Cleo and Demon were in a relationship. Then again, why should she be privy to this information? They didn't go out of their way to keep it a secret, but they didn't advertise, either. They rarely indulged in more than a hug publicly.

Another thing that struck Zahra was how Simone had misinterpreted something that was very important to Demon. When Zahra first joined the group, Demon had given her two books to read. One was about the civil war. The other was a collection of Fred Hampton speeches. Head tried to tell her what to expect in one of these books, and Demon stopped him, saying, "No, let her read it for herself. That's another problem with the way we get our information. We're always willing to let someone tell us something we should research on our own." On another occasion, he'd told her, "You need to look up this case and do your own research before we get there. Don't never let someone tell you how you should feel about something – not even if it's me."

This didn't sound like someone who liked to do the thinking for others. But maybe Zahra was being defensive.

She asked Simone, "Why do you feel like Demon wants to do the thinking for us?"

"He making all the decisions," Simone quipped. "What you call that?"

"What decisions did he make that you were against? Other than killing that boy?"

Simone's eyes narrowed, making Zahra feel like she should come clean about their relationship.

"Let me guess," Simone said, "you was one of the ones who voted for the calling card."

"Well, yeah. Most of the group did."

"*All* of the group didn't. Just like *all* of the group didn't want to kill that boy, and *all* of the group didn't wanna make that video. It's cool if you was one of the ones who did. That don't change nothing about what we doing tonight – except that you and me gotta get on the same page about that little girl."

"I don't want to harm that girl," Zahra reiterated. "If we can come up with a plan to avoid it, I'm all for it."

"I'll figure something out," Simone said, her eyes back on the restaurant. "Let me ask you another question, since you seem to be Team Demon."

Zahra chuckled at how inadvertently accurate that term was. She said, "Sure."

"Does it bother you that the only reason this man is about to die is because of what we did to the militia?"

Simone wasn't wrong about that. Their target was a 43-year-old man named Jason Bearfield. He was selected for execution after connecting with extremists online and expressing his desire to carry out a shooting against black people. He'd hidden his identity on the underground message board, but Head and Einstein frequented those websites as often as the racists who felt comfortable there.

Once a viable threat had been identified, they could track the user's IP address and eventually match that information to a real person. A surveillance team was tasked with putting eyes on people like Bearfield to determine if their internet boasting was all talk, or if they had the means (or were in the process of acquiring the means) to carry out their online threats. In this case, they confirmed that Bearfield was a problem. Within the past eight days, he had purchased two assault-style rifles and tons of ammunition.

"Just because he said he wants to do this for the militia," Zahra told Simone, "doesn't mean it's true. He could've been harboring these feelings for a long time."

"Cleo," Simone said, shaking her head, "I know you got the same intel I got. This man ain't never said nothing like that on the internet until *after* Demon's video came out. I know you support him, but it's okay to admit that maybe he was wrong for posting that video. He was wrong about leaving that stupid card too. When these folks was dropping dead, and nobody was connecting the murders, nobody was targeting us. Now we gotta deal with the police, these militias, and random *sympathizers*," she said, nodding towards the restaurant. "If we didn't catch on to this dude, we'd have blood on our hands. Demon would, for sure. That's why I voted against the calling card. I would've voted against the video too, if he gave us a chance."

Zahra had never met anyone in the group who openly stated which way they voted on the calling card.

She told her, "Throughout our history, every time black people stand up for something, black people die as a result of it. Does that mean we should never take a stand?"

"I ain't say that."

"Well, let me ask you this," Zahra said. "If you voted against the calling card and would've voted against the video, why didn't you text Demon and tell him you wanted out of the group?"

Simone's expression hardened. "Because I don't have to agree with everything our leaders do to support the cause. I had a lot of reasons to join this group. The shooting in Charleston is the main one. That coward went in there and prayed with them people. They welcomed him with open arms. They didn't ask what this crazy-ass white boy was doing there. They welcomed him, because that's what Christians do. Then he pulled out a gun and laid waste to what was supposed to be holy ground. Malcolm X used to say the white man is the devil. They hated him for saying that, but what that look like to you? If that ain't the devil, then there's no such thing.

"I'll always be down with the Ace of Spades, because this the first group I ever met that understands that you don't reason with the devil. Ain't no trying to understand why a snake keeps biting you. *It's a fucking snake.* It ain't gon' stop biting till you cut its head off. I don't have to agree with every decision Demon and them make to agree that they right about the final solution. You understand that?"

Zahra nodded. "Yeah. I do."

"Good," Simone said, watching their target, "'cause this asshole is getting ready to leave, and we still ain't figured out how we can kill him without killing his daughter."

∞ ∞ ∞ ∞ ∞ ∞ ∞

After leaving the restaurant, they trailed the target for fifteen minutes, until Bearfield turned into his suburban neighborhood. Confident that he was headed home, the female assassins continued on the main thoroughfare. They headed for a nearby business district and found a parking garage where they could begin the waiting game without arousing suspicion from passing motorists. It was summertime, so it was impossible to predict when Bearfield's daughter might go to bed that night, but her father had to show up for work bright and early tomorrow morning. It was currently 9 pm.

While they waited, the ladies talked more. Zahra found that when Simone wasn't being contentious, she had a pleasant personality. She told Zahra about her humble upbringing in Michigan and how she never imagined one day becoming an activist or a revolutionary – definitely not a murderer – until the need to become these things was thrust upon her. Despite having a large family that was well-connected, Simone easily made the decision to separate from her loved ones when she was approached by a stranger in the parking lot of her apartment complex.

"Demon don't know how close he was to getting pepper sprayed," she reflected amusingly. "I'm glad I took the time to see what he was talking about."

In turn, Zahra reminisced about her grandmother. Simone was aware of the shooting that took her life. In the beginning, Zahra couldn't get through the story of what had occurred in that Walmart without being brought to tears. But she could now. She wondered if this was because she was doing something about it. Most would say she was dealing with her trauma in an unhealthy manner, but most people hadn't suffered the trauma she had.

Zahra also felt the need to clear up the misconception she and her accomplice had.

"You didn't know me and Demon are together?"

In the darkness of the car, Simone watched her eyes. She shook her head. "No. I didn't know that." She thought for a second and then asked, "Does it make you feel some kind of way, the things I said about him?"

"No. I understand that not everybody in the group agrees with him."

"You gon' tell him what I said?"

Zahra shook her head. "He already knows. Maybe not about you personally, but he knows some members have been complaining."

Simone shrugged. "I don't care if you tell him. I didn't say anything I wouldn't say to his face. I got no problem speaking my mind."

"Yeah," Zahra said smiling. "I can see that."

"I appreciate you telling me, though," Simone said. "Glad I didn't say that nigga was ugly, or nothing like that."

That brought a chuckle from her new friend.

"I'm happy for you," Simone decided. "Him too. Everybody need somebody."

Zahra nodded. "Yeah, that's what they say."

∞ ∞ ∞ ∞ ∞ ∞ ∞

They left the parking garage at one a.m. There was a chance the daughter might still be awake at that hour, but her father shouldn't be. Before leaving the garage, Zahra had asked once again about the plan for the girl if she became an obstacle to the mission.

Simone told her, "I'm hoping she in bed. If so, I'ma make sure she get some *real* good sleep."

"How you gon' do that?"

"I'm good with chemicals," Simone replied vaguely. "Prolly could'a been an anesthesiologist, if life hadn't led me down this other road."

Zahra remained curious but didn't pose any follow up questions.

Go-time began the moment they returned to the target's neighborhood. To gain entry into the home, the ladies opted for the garage, which had already been compromised. Two days ago, one of their operatives stopped by Bearfield's home armed with a gadget that had been designed by Einstein. From the back of the house, he used the remote to reset the garage door opener. He then planted a small camera on a utility pole to the right of the house.

When Bearfield arrived at his home later that day, the clicker in his car did not work. As most homeowners would, he simply got out of his truck and used the panel on the outside of the garage to gain entry. Once inside, he reset his clicker. Problem solved. Bearfield never took the time to investigate how the opener had been reset. He was also unaware of the camera that was facing the panel he'd just used.

He had unwittingly given his killers the code.

The assassins drove through the alley behind Bearfield's home and parked in the driveway. Zahra exited the car and used the panel to open the garage. The sound of the metal door rolling up the tracks was not too loud, but it wasn't silent either. If Bearfield or his daughter was up and alert, they would have heard it. The ladies had their pistols up in the firing position as they entered the house through the back door. It seemed as if everyone left that door unlocked.

Moving quickly, they checked the living room. The lights were off. It was clear. The adjacent kitchen, same findings, lights off, clear. There was no one in the dining room. They turned down the main hallway. Ahead of them, light illuminated under the door of the master bedroom. It was too dim to be the bedroom light. Zahra guessed it was coming from the bathroom. They were silent as they checked the doors to their right and left. The first bedroom was empty. The guest bathroom was empty. In the third room, there was a body on the bed. They could tell from the long, blonde hair that this was the daughter. Thankfully, she was asleep. Simone signaled for Zahra to hold her position as she crept inside the room. Zahra kept her gun trained on the door ahead of her. She stole glances at her partner.

Simone holstered her weapon as she sneaked into the room. She reached into her pockets and removed two items. One was a small towel. The other was a plastic bottle. She squirted the contents of the bottle onto the towel before returning the bottle to her pocket. By then, she was standing over the bed. She took a moment to plan her attack before pouncing with the nimbleness of a feline. She used her legs and free arm to pin the girl under her sheets. With her other hand, she mashed the towel over the teen's mouth and nose. Bearfield's daughter never had a chance to cry out for help.

Zahra didn't know what was on the towel, but the teenager's thrashing gradually ceased in less than twenty seconds. Simone held the towel in place a few moments more before climbing off the bed. She stuffed the towel in her back pocket and drew her gun as she approached Zahra, who was both surprised and impressed by what she'd seen.

"Come on," Simone whispered, and they got moving again.

With both women prepared for whatever they might encounter behind the next door, Zahra turned the knob slowly before pushing it in just as quietly. No one inside the room stirred. The women stepped inside quickly, scanning their gun in all directions. The bed had either not been made that day, or someone had been in it recently. The room was empty. Their attention was drawn to the bathroom, where, as Zahra had expected, the only light in the room shone under the closed door. They moved in that direction.

As they drew nearer, they shot each other perplexed glances. There were sounds coming from inside. *Sex* sounds. Zahra reached for the doorknob and turned it slowly. Once again, it was not locked. She pushed the door open forcefully, revealing a brightly lit bathroom and their target.

"*Janie! No!*"

Bearfield was butt naked. He stood facing the sink with his cellphone in one hand and his rock-hard dick in the other. The stroking hand glistened with what Zahra assumed was lotion. Simone crowded the doorway so she could get a look. The killers wore all black, including their ski masks. Bearfield was stunned stiff. Realizing intruders had caught him in this private act rather than his daughter didn't make him feel any better.

Zahra tilted her head slightly. She stepped further into the room to allow Simone space to enter.

Bearfield found his voice. "*What the, what the hell you doing here?*" he panted. He was a bearded man in okay shape, except for an oversized belly.

"I think you know what this is," Zahra told him. "Don't do nothing stupid."

"Now, I done heard of catching a nigga with his pants down," Simone said, "but I ain't never seen no shit like this."

"Put your phone down," Zahra instructed him. "You can, um, you can keep yo dick in yo hand."

Bearfield's face had gone from pasty pale to beet red in a matter of seconds. "I, I know what this is. I know who you are."

"*Put the phone down!*" Zahra barked.

She was surprised the man didn't try to turn it off before complying. The sound of the video he'd been watching continued to play. Zahra was confused about what she was hearing. The barrel of her gun remained trained on the target's chest as she took a peek at his phone.

"Girl, you ain't gon' believe this."

"What?" Simone said. She came closer so she could see what Zahra saw. Her eyes widened. "Ain't this some shit. You in here watching *gay* porn?"

"*Black* gay porn," Zahra noted. "That's what get you off?"

"Oh shit, I just had an epiphany," Simone said, her eyes widening. "He hate black people 'cause he in the closet, and he can't get nobody to stick a black dick in his ass!"

She laughed hoarsely. Zahra couldn't help but chuckle too.

"Where's Janie," the man said his voice rattling. "What'd you do to her?" He had let go of his dick by then but made no other moves.

"I guess the rumors are true," Simone said, looking down at his swollen, pink piece. "You white boys ain't packing *at all*."

"Wh, where's my daughter? What'd you do to her?"

"She fine," Zahra said. "She sleep."

"*You're lying*," he growled. "I know what y'all did in North Dakota. You killed that boy. *What'd you do to my little girl*?" He was pleading now. The range of emotions he'd experienced since they entered the bathroom was fascinating.

"She telling the truth," Simone said. "I know you ain't got no reason to believe us, but that's your only option. You not gon' be able to leave this bathroom to go check on her. But I promise you, your daughter is fine."

Bearfield's eyes darted from one intruder to the other. A moment later, his expression shifted again. The tense muscles in his face loosened. He closed his eyes and took a deep breath. He blew it out slowly through his nostrils. He shook his head and opened his eyes. "Y'all here because of the internet, right?"

Simone shrugged.

Zahra nodded.

"They, uh..." He coughed and then cleared his throat. "I was worried that wasn't a safe place to talk. How'd you find me?"

"I think I'd rather send you to hell still wondering about that," Zahra replied.

"Well, um." He swallowed and took another deep breath. "Can I, can you answer one question?"

Zahra told him, "Maybe."

"After what y'all did, you didn't think somebody like me was gonna take revenge? You don't think y'all deserve it?"

Zahra thought the question would feed into the things her partner had said earlier. She was surprised to hear Simone's response.

"The revenge game didn't start in North Dakota, asshole. It started on those slave ships. You wanna get revenge on *us* because we got a little revenge on *y'all*? What kind of sense that make? What you should've done when you heard about North Dakota was take a step back and *think*, really think about why that happened. Then you should've told yourself, '*After all we did to them people, we deserve that.*' Instead, you put yourself in this situation."

Zahra wanted to do the honors, but Simone gunned the man down the moment she was done speaking. Though the silenced reports weren't loud, they were unexpected and jarring. Once her brain caught up to what had just occurred, Zahra stepped over the body to admire her partner's handiwork. Bearfield's eyes were as big as quarters. He was gasping for air that wouldn't have helped him if he was able to suck it down. The holes in his chest were still smoking. She didn't have to finish him off, but she did. A bullet in the face brought the gasping to an abrupt end. She removed a playing card from her pocket and tossed it onto the corpse.

The women left the bathroom. Zahra looked back when she heard the door close. Simone had done that. Zahra watched as her partner checked the knob to make sure she'd locked it.

Looking back at Zahra, she said, "I'm doing this for the girl. Seeing something like that will stay with her forever."

Simone reached into her pocket for another card. She hesitated and then produced the rest of the cards she was carrying. She tossed them on the floor in front of the door. There were ten in all.

"You think that'll stop her from trying to kick in the door tomorrow morning?"

Zahra knew Simone was compassionate, but this level of empathy was unexpected. "It should. By now, everybody know about the Ace of Spades."

Simone sighed. "Well, it's the best I can do. If she see the door locked, and see them cards, and *still* force her way in, that's on her."

They paused at the teenager's door on the way out of the house. The girl was snoring loudly, very much alive, for better or worse.

∞ ∞ ∞ ∞ ∞ ∞ ∞

That night, Demon and Zahra shared a bed at the tactical point. While cuddling, they discussed the success of their missions. Demon and Jewell had put down three enemies. Zahra was jealous. She did not tell him what Simone had said about him, but she told him about the measures they'd taken to spare the daughter. Demon wasn't surprised by this.

"Simone got a good heart," he said. "She one of the good ones."

Zahra frowned slightly in the darkness. Surely Demon knew that Simone had been part of the one-third who voted against his plan to leave a calling card.

He asked her, "Does this mean you changed your mind about working with other people? It don't have to be just me and you all the time?"

"I guess so. I liked working with Simone. I wouldn't mind if we hooked up again."

"Pretty sure I can make that happen."

He didn't speak again. A few moments later, Zahra realized he'd fallen asleep. She closed her eyes and quickly followed suit.

It had been a long day.

CHAPTER EIGHT
I SEE WHITE PEOPLE

As the Ace of Spades continued to adjust to the aftermath of Demon's *Strange Fruit* video, their leader kept his foot on the gas with the recruitment drive. In the first week of August, he brought three new soldiers to tactical points in Baton Rouge, Chicago and Salt Lake City.

The first had been given the name JT. For his initiation, JT sniped a skinhead in Arizona who was out for a leisurely stroll with his girlfriend. Demon named the second recruit Groucho, because he didn't believe the man was capable of smiling. Groucho got up close and personal with his initiation. He first shot and then strangled the number two man in Waco's Son's of Liberty faction. The third recruit, aptly named Pyro, set fire to a house in New Orleans. The homeowner had organized a chapter of the White Trash Rebels and hosted their meetings in his backyard. In addition to the target's death, his three dogs and pet python were killed in the blaze. Pyro later said he felt sorry about killing the animals.

Demon told him, "Don't feel bad. War ain't never pretty. It is what it is."

Given all that he'd learned about these recruits and how they'd proven themselves, Demon expected them to be welcomed with open arms.

They were not.

Their white skin garnished suspicious stares when Demon brought them to the tactical points. He did not address the members who were taken aback by the pale skin in their midst, but he hated that the recruits had to experience that.

Undaunted, one week later he brought in three more new faces, this time to the Houston headquarters. By then, Demon was prepared for the looks of uncertainty these men received when he introduced them to the members who were present that day. Not surprisingly, one of the dark faces that didn't attempt to hide their disdain belonged to Cujo. Demon didn't wait for his brooding counterpart to call him to one of the back rooms to voice his displeasure.

He told the new recruits, "Hey, I'll be back in a second. Y'all make yourselves at home," and then he stepped to Cujo directly. "Hey, what's up, man. You wanna holler at me?"

"Yeah," Cujo said, his eyes on the white men.

"Come on," Demon said, leading the way down the hallway. "Let's get this over with."

Demon chuckled humorlessly when they entered the bedroom. He told Cujo, "I don't hate no part of this house, but I'm starting to not like this room. How many times have we been in her disagreeing about something?"

Cujo closed the door and then turned to face him. "You the one who called me in here."

"Don't act like this wasn't finna happen. I'm just cutting to the chase."

Cujo frowned at that.

"Go 'head, man," Demon insisted. "Speak your piece."

"Fine. What's up with these white folks, Demon? I heard about the ones you brought in last week. Now you got three more. And you brought them to our *headquarters*. Our whole operation is in jeopardy if the wrong people find out about this place."

"Every member of our group has been to this house. These men have a right to be here. Since when did you become a *racist*? Our enemies are racist. We ain't never had no rule that say we don't bring in white people."

"We never had a rule because it's never come up. But if I had known you were planning to do something like this, then yeah, I think we would've had a talk about whether it should be allowed or not."

"First of all, I asked you if you wanted to be part of recruiting. You said no, so you can't come in on the back end and tell me how to do it."

Cujo's eyes narrowed.

"Second," Demon continued, "those white boys have done everything possible to prove themselves. They as straight as everybody else I recruited."

"Just because they popped their cherry don't mean we can trust them."

"Look, man, I understand why some of our members are unsure about what they're seeing. Our enemies are white, and now some of these new recruits are white. On the surface level, that looks like a conflict of interests. But you know the history of our people's struggle as much as I do. You know about Viola Liuzzo, Michael Henry Schwerner, Andrew Goodman – *Reverend Klunder*, that man literally got ran over by a *bulldozer* while trying to stop them crackers from building a white-only school.

"White people been shedding blood for us for years. Hell, the original abolitionists were damn near *all white*. You think it was only black people on the streets with them Black Lives Matters protests? Don't' forget, all three of the men Kyle Rittenhouse shot were *white*. Antifa want the same thing we want, and they hate the same people we hate. Makes sense to bring people like that onboard."

Flustered, Cujo asked, "Is that who you recruiting? *Antifa?*"

"Some of 'em, yeah. But what's important is the way you reacting. You should be out there shaking their hands. You should be pulling the other members to the side and giving them a history lesson, instead of allowing their ignorance to create uncertainty in our group. Shit, you not just allowing it. You right along with 'em."

Cujo sighed gruffly. "Alright, Demon. If this what we're doing, it is what it is. But, *as usual*, I wish you would'a told me first."

"With all due respect, I don't need you micromanaging me. I don't do that to you. When you tell me you setting up a new tactical point, I trust that it's gon' get done, and it's gon' be straight. Soon as I brought these recruits here, you should'a known that I wouldn't do that unless they was straight."

"That's a lot of trust you want me to give you."

"Well, hell," Demon said, throwing up his hands. "If I ain't earned your trust by now by now, I never will. I'll holler at you later."

He stepped past him and left the room.

Demon headed straight for the computer room, where another crisis was unfolding.

"*Man, fuck!*" Einstein exclaimed as he furiously manipulated applications on his PC. "I'm fucking sick of this shit!"

"Damn, what's wrong, man?" Demon's eyes were filled with concern as he approached him.

"They got my IP address!" Einstein said, his eyes on his monitor. *"Again!"*

"Huh?" Demon stepped closer and studied his screen, but he had no idea what he was looking at.

"It's okay," Head told him. "Just make a new one. I'll get started on another VPN."

Einstein turned on him with fire in his eyes. "I know I can make a new address, and you know that's not the point! Somebody's in my shit, and I hate people digging in my shit! If nobody else in this house knows how much I hate that, you do!"

"They got me a couple of weeks ago," Head reminded him. "I got past it, and you can too. Just a little setback."

"Man, don't even..."

Einstein's hand was balled into a fist. Demon didn't think the computer geeks would ever come to blows, but he placed himself between them, just in case.

"What is going on?" he asked. "What you mean they got your IP address? Who?"

"I don't know," Einstein cried. "Could be the feds or some damn militia hacker."

Realizing the seriousness of this breach, Demon asked, "What can they do with your IP address? Is that something that can lead them to this house?"

"No," Einstein said. "Not exactly. It'll reveal a general location. They can probably tell what city we're in, but not the address to this house. We're safe, as far as that's concerned."

Demon didn't feel very safe at all.

"The worst part is, they can tell what I've been doing with my computer," Einstein continued. "That's the bigger problem. If it's some random hacker who don't know what they're looking for, it's no big deal. But if it's the feds, then they know the IP address most likely belongs to someone in the Ace of Spades."

Demon stared at him, unblinking.

"It's not the end of the world," Head said. "They already know we out here, and they know what we do with our computers. They always trying to find us, it's just that lately they been trying *extra* hard."

"You said they got your IP address too?" Demon asked him.

"Yeah, but I already took care of it. We just gotta do better with our VPN. They figuring out ways around it."

Demon was lost. "What's a VPN?"

"Virtual Private Network," Einstein said. "It's what we use to do our business on the internet without anyone knowing who's doing it."

"How'd they get past it?"

"Hackers always find a way," Head told him.

"And as far as your IP address," Demon said to Einstein, "you said they can tell what you've been doing on your computer?"

"Not everything. But they can see a lot, if they know what they're doing."

Demon nodded. A cold chill had enveloped him. "Are you sure they can't use any of that information to locate us?"

Einstein shook his head. "No. If they could, I'd be running out of this house by now. After all we've done, everybody in this group is getting a mandatory life sentence if they catch us."

Demon thought he was lowballing that prediction. Most members of the group would get the death penalty if they were ever found out.

"So, we good?" he asked. "Y'all got this taken care of?"

"Yeah, we good," Einstein said. "I just don't like this *invasion of privacy* feeling."

If this wasn't such a tense topic, Demon would've pointed out the irony in his comment. From sun up to sun down, all the computer guys did was invade people's privacy.

"Alright," he said. "I know y'all got a lot of work to do, so I'll leave you to it."

When he turned to leave the room, Demon saw Cujo standing in the doorway. He sighed inwardly, his eyes narrowing. *Nope*, he said to himself as he approached his partner. *I'm not doing this again.*

Cujo must have read his mind. Rather than instigate another argument, he stepped aside and allowed Demon to pass.

∞ ∞ ∞ ∞ ∞ ∞ ∞

The following Friday, Demon and Zahra racked up more air miles. This time their destination was Nashville, Tennessee. At one a.m., they sat in a dark-colored Tahoe down the street from a bar called Tennessee Taproom. Nearly a dozen Harley's lined the street in front of the establishment. Seeing the bikes made Demon less comfortable than he already was about their Tahoe. If someone hopped on one of those bad boys and gave chase, they wouldn't be able to outrun them in this boat. The only reason he opted for the roomier vehicle was because he and Zahra were not alone on this mission.

Redd sat behind him as quiet and focused as ever. Demon hadn't worked with Redd in a while, but he had full confidence in him. The fourth soldier was a new recruit named Hulk. Zahra thought Demon was getting less inventive with his nicknames, but Hulk liked the moniker. He was a 260-pound stocky fellow, mostly muscle. Demon's second option was *Cornfed*, but he didn't want anyone in the group to take that to mean Hulk was an unintelligent hillbilly. He had actually graduated near the top of his high school class and attended Michigan State on a wrestling scholarship. After college, he found success in real estate and could've continued pursuing the American Dream if his conscious had not been bombarded by all of the hashtags.

#philandocastile

#breonnataylor
#sandrabland
#ericgarner
#georgefloyd
#tyrenichols

Hulk connected with other likeminded individuals who believed they should take a stand for black people. No one in his family (that he knew of) was racist, but most thought his decision was odd. Despite his family's objections, Hulk followed his heart and found himself at protests in places like Minneapolis, Memphis, Los Angeles, and Charlottesville. He never became a member of Antifa. As far as he knew, Antifa was more of a philosophy, than an organization. But that was the label the media pinned on him and his counterparts.

Black protesters were rioters.

White protesters were Antifa.

Like most people, Hulk was both dismayed and riveted the first time he saw Demon's *Strange Fruit* video. He followed a lot of online chatter and realized that the people who hated the video the most were the same people he'd been protesting against for the past few years. He began to defend the video, which led to plenty of wonderful online arguments. Gradually, he feared his reckless exercise of free speech might land him in real-world trouble, so he toned down his rhetoric.

But it was too late.

One month ago, a stranger approached him in the parking lot of Walmart. The man told him flat out, "I been seeing the things you're saying online. And I know you been going to those BLM protests..."

Hulk almost shit his pants. He thought the man was a federal agent. He later learned that the man went by *Demon*, and he was responsible for the most sensational video Hulk had ever seen. A week later, Hulk got his affairs in order and gave Demon a call. The following day, he and Demon caught a flight. That same night, Hulk popped his cherry by shooting an unarmed man in the face. The man didn't look like a white supremacist, but Hulk had done his research at the airport. He understood why Demon wanted the man to die.

That murder was the most horrible thing Adrian Turney had ever done. But he did not regret it. With that murder, Adrian received a new name and membership into a group that was doing things Antifa could only dream of.

Tonight, he was grateful for the opportunity to prove himself again.

He sat in the back of the Tahoe wearing all black. This was the first time he'd ever worn a ski mask. In his lap, he cradled an AR-15. The weapon had been converted to fire fully automatic, which was illegal, but everything the Ace of Spades did was illegal. Hulk listened closely as their leader gave the final instructions.

"It's prolly gon' be some innocent people who die in there," Demon told them. "I hope it ain't more than a few, but I know it'll be more than one. I just got a text from intel. As usual, the Aryan Brotherhood took over the bar tonight. It's about 15 people in there. Two of 'em are women. The gang damn near ran my guy outta there, talking 'bout, '*You sure you in the right place?*' You know, that kinda shit. The bar owner is a member, so he's good to go. But the females may be bystanders. They might be members of the group, but I can't say for sure. Either way, I don't want y'all holding back because of them. If you hesitate, they'll have time to react."

"So basically," Redd said, "we need to lay down everything in that joint."

Demon nodded. "Any of y'all got a problem with that?"

No one did.

He locked eyes with Hulk in the rearview mirror. "What about you, newbie? If your conscious gon' be kicking yo ass later, you can hang out in the car while we take care of this. I won't hold it against you."

"No, I'm good," Hulk said. "Aryans and Aryan sympathizers are the same thing, as far as I'm concerned."

"Alright," Demon said. "We taking off in one minute. Everybody mask up. Soon as I hit the brakes, bail out and take care of business. Shouldn't take no more than two minutes. Police response time in this area is seven minutes."

The two guys in the back, already had their masks on. That only left Zahra and Demon, who had to put on theirs. Demon pulled the cloth over his head and adjusted the eye sockets. He looked over at his woman and waited for her to nod before he put the SUV in drive. They were three blocks away from the bar. Demon usually liked to go in hot and heavy, but he did not speed to the target. He didn't want anyone to notice anything suspicious until it was too late.

∞ ∞ ∞ ∞ ∞ ∞ ∞

The moment he stopped in front of the bar, all four occupants sprang from it as if they'd been ejected. The front door of the establishment was open. Without a word, they stormed inside with their weapons at the ready. Demon was already shooting as he moved to the left. Zahra was right behind him. Her rifle roared as she went right. Redd took position in the middle left, and Hulk completed the firing line at middle right.

The racket of all four guns firing simultaneously was enormous. The carnage the bullets caused was a slap to the face of anyone who believed assault rifles were not weapons of mass destruction. Zahra saw white faces explode in a spray of pink mist. Limbs were nearly torn from torsos. Bodies twisted in splashes of blood like they were being electrocuted. No one was spared. Few had time to scream. Flesh and brain matter decorated the walls. The team kept firing. The whites kept dying. Glass and furniture shattered. Only the bartender had time to consider reaching for a weapon. Zahra was about to take him out when his throat exploded. The force of the bullets slamming into him sent him crashing into his liquor display.

Only Hulk saw one patron make a run for it. The man had been standing just to the right of the door. All of the killers had stepped past him before they opened fire. The man stood in stunned shock for nearly ten seconds before he got his legs working. Hulk took off right behind him. When the fire ceased, the three remaining gunmen raced back to the Tahoe. It was then that they saw Hulk booking it up the street.

Watching the two men run, Demon thought there was no way Hulk would catch him, and he was a fool for trying. The man being chased was thinner and quicker, and he was running for his life, which is one hell of a motivation. Demon thought Hulk should hold his position and open fire. No one can outrun a bullet.

But Hulk did catch him. Even while carrying the rifle, he sprinted fast enough to throw a swooping kick that caught the other man on the ankle. The runner lost his balance and tumbled forward on the hard street. He and Hulk were a few blocks away from the others by then. They all watched, waiting for Hulk to seal the deal. But Hulk didn't start shooting. They knew he was saying something to the other man, but from that distance, they couldn't make out what it was.

"The fuck he doing?" Redd said. "We gotta go!"

"Get in," Demon instructed them. "We'll pick him up."

They piled back into the Tahoe and made it to Hulk in time to see the downed man crawling across the street. Hulk kept his gun trained on his back. With the windows down, they could hear what Hulk was saying now.

"Put your teeth on that curb. Open your mouth wide!"

"*Please don't do this!*" the man cried. "*I didn't do nothing! I don't know what this is about!*"

"*Shut up and do it!*" Hulk kicked him in the ass to get him moving. "You wanna live, or you wanna die?"

"Man, I'm finna go get this fool," Redd said.

Demon stopped him before he got out of the truck. "Hold up. Let him finish."

"*We running out of time,*" Redd complained. "Police gon' be here any minute."

"We got time," Demon said. "Just, give 'em a minute..."

Zahra had seen *American History X*. The scene Hulk was reenacting was the most gut-wrenching part of the movie. Some have described it as the hardest part to watch of any movie *ever*. After seeing it on Netflix, Zahra had told herself that no one would ever open their mouth and place their teeth on the curb, knowing what was about to occur. As she watched Hulk, she realized self-preservation trumps all. The target had seen what happened in the club. There was no doubt his pursuers had the will and means to murder him if he did not comply.

When the sobbing man was in position, Zahra cringed as Hulk raised his big boot over the back of his head.

She could not look away.

She winced when the heavy foot came down with a hard thud.

The sound of teeth scraping and breaking on the curb would remain in her psyche for the rest of her life. Blood flowed like a broken water line.

The victim did not physically react to the trauma – not like she expected. His body went completely limp. Zahra thought Hulk had broken his neck. Their new recruit put a bullet in the back of the man's head, just in case. Despite all she'd seen since she joined the Ace of Spades, Zahra was appalled.

"*God damn,*" Redd breathed as Hulk turned and headed for the Tahoe.

For half a second, Zahra hoped Demon would speed away before he got inside. Increasing the group's membership was important, but did they want people like this eating, and sleeping, and *being* right next to them?

But Demon said, "I knew he was a good one," and Zahra knew that he would not speed away.

As they fled the scene, Hulk could not contain his excitement. Panting, he ran his fingers through his blonde hair, which was unkempt after snatching off the ski mask.

"Did y'all see that? I did 'em just like the movie. *Just like they did to the guy in that movie!*"

Demon was the only one with the wherewithal to respond.

"Yeah, we seen it. You did good, man. That's the shit I'm talking about. That's how you make a statement..."

CHAPTER NINE
ALIASES

Two weeks later, Zahra sat at a small table at The Old Spaghetti Factory in Salt Lake City. Across from her, a man named Bob Dennard grinned eagerly. They had not yet ordered their meal, but judging by the look on Dennard's face, the date was going wonderfully. On the contrary, Zahra was starting to think she should cut the encounter short. She thought Dennard could be the poster child for *thirsty*. She wondered what she'd missed and how she'd missed it. Flashbacks of the incident at Charley's Steakhouse made her underarms feel damp. She cradled her purse in her lap. It was unzipped. Her hand was partly inside. The feel of the .44 magnum moderately alleviated her tension.

Since joining the group, Zahra had completed multiple solo missions. But this was the first time she'd attempted a recruitment on her own. She thought she'd done her due diligence when vetting Dennard, but something about this guy wasn't right. She couldn't stop thinking about what she'd told Demon when they ran into trouble in Tampa.

David, I don't know if I should be recruiting people. This, this might be too much for me.

His assurances gave her the confidence to get back on the bike. Now, not only had the feeling of failure returned, but it was accompanied by a sense of danger. She looked around, making sure her surroundings had not changed, and the restaurant's exit remained accessible. Dennard drew her attention back to him.

"So, are you with the Ace of Spades?"

He'd leaned closer and posed the question with a hushed tone, but Zahra felt like he had *screamed* the name of the group in the moderately populated restaurant.

"Don't say that," she warned him. "Someone might hear you."

"Oh, I'm sorry. I'm just curious. When you contacted me, that's the first thing that came to mind. I've been following – um, *that group* – and I've always wanted to meet someone who is a part of it. I was hoping that was you..."

Zahra shook her head slowly. Her Spidey senses made the hairs stand on the back of her neck. She thought back to what her first encounter with Demon was like. She recalled being more curious than anything. It was possible that with the notoriety of their group, some candidates would jump to conclusions early on in the recruitment process. But Dennard was a little *too* excited about his assumption. Zahra would've preferred if he was guarded and apprehensive about the unknown.

"I never said I was part of any group," she told him. "I told you that I saw some of the things you were fighting for on Twitter, and maybe we could get together to do something about it."

"Right. And I'm ready," he said nodding. "Sign me up for whatever you have in mind."

Dennard was in his mid-thirties. His glasses were stylish. He wore khakis with a short-sleeved button down. He was as handsome as the picture on his driver's license. What the license hadn't shown was the cunning in his eyes. There was a chance that there was nothing untoward about this man, but Zahra was rarely mistaken when she trusted her instincts. If she was wrong about him, the worst that could happen is they would lose out on a new member. But if she was right...

"What I had in mind was starting a petition," she told him. "I was thinking we could take it to the mayor and demand better training for the police. If that didn't work, we could try to organize a protest."

Dennard's smile wavered. "Oh. Is that it?"

"You don't think that would work?"

"Here, in Salt Lake City? We haven't had any problems with the police, not recently. On Twitter, I was responding to events that made *national news*. I was talking about the white nationalists, what they've been doing to your people. I thought you wanted to meet to talk about that. I want to do something about the hate crimes against black people..."

"You don't think police brutality is a hate crime against black people?"

"Well, yeah. I mean, sure it is. I was just..." He shrugged. "I thought you'd want to go after the bigger fish and really do something about it – something more than protesting. That's what I thought you wanted to talk about."

"You thought I was part of a group that's hurting people," Zahra said, looking around again. "I'm not. I don't want to hurt anybody. I'm sorry I wasted your time. I'm gonna leave."

She rose from her seat.

Dennard almost got shot in the face when he grabbed her hand to stop her.

"Wait."

She pulled away from him forcefully. "What are you doing? Don't touch me."

He recoiled. "I'm sorry. I didn't mean any harm. I don't want you to leave. We can talk about the petition or protest. That's a start. I'm willing to start there."

She shook her head. "No, I think it's better if I go."

"Please, wait."

"Look, Bob, I had the wrong idea about you, and you definitely have the wrong idea about me. If you want to get into some social activism, go ahead. You don't need me for that. I wish you the best."

She started towards the door but thought better of it. She looked around and made a show of asking the nearest waiter, "Where's the bathroom?"

"It's right over here," the man said and pointed.

Zahra headed that way and found an empty stall when she was inside. She didn't pull her jeans down before sitting on the toilet seat. Her mind raced. She checked the time, knowing it was better to rely on the clock, rather than her impression of how long she planned to wait. After a full ten minutes, she left the bathroom. If Dennard was still at the table, he'd probably think she was unwell. But their table was empty. A busser was removing the drinking glasses, in preparation for the next patron.

Zahra breathed a sigh of relief.

But when she emerged from the restaurant, a cursory glance around the parking lot revealed the recruit's car. It was right where he had parked thirty minutes ago. She had allowed him to arrive first, as Demon had taught her. From across the street, she'd watched him enter the restaurant. She'd waited five minutes before she met him inside. She'd followed Demon's instructions precisely, but somewhere along the way, she'd missed *something*.

She did not stare at Dennard's car or acknowledge that she'd seen him. It was dark, so it was unlikely that he'd seen her eyes briefly settle on his Altima. She tried to appear unbothered as she got into her car, started it, and backed out of the parking spot. She told herself that there was a chance she was wrong. Maybe he was just checking messages on his phone.

But when she pulled out of the restaurant's parking lot, Dennard's headlights came on. She watched him in the rearview mirror as she turned onto the main thoroughfare. Dennard caught up with her and made the same turn.

∞ ∞ ∞ ∞ ∞ ∞ ∞

After driving a couple of miles and confirming she was being followed, Zahra made the call.

"Hey, what's up?" Demon answered.

"Something's wrong." Now that she was in her car, she felt as if she had a little more control over the situation, especially with her man's voice booming through the speakers.

"What's the problem?"

"The guy I went to meet today is following me. He knows about us. He thinks I'm part of the group."

"What? How the hell you let that happen?"

She told him all that had transpired up to that point.

"You vetted him yourself?" Demon asked.

"Yes."

"What's the name?"

"Bob Dennard."

"You got his license?"

"I'm texting it to you now."

Demon told her, "Hold on, let me get Einstein on the line with us..."

Half a minute of silence passed before he spoke again. "Alight, Cleo, you there?"

"Yeah."

"Okay. I got Einstein."

"Hey, Cleo," the computer guy said.

"Hey," she breathed.

"I checked that license you sent Demon. Something ain't adding up. I looked up Bob Dennard's license from DPS. The picture on it doesn't match the picture on the one you have. Everything on your license is the same except the picture. And the description doesn't match. Bob Dennard has brown eyes, but the guy on your license has blue eyes..."

Zahra felt like her intestines were writhing like a snake den. *"Fuck."* How did she miss that?

"He gave you a fake ID for sure," Einstein continued. "Let me guess, you did a background check on *Bob Dennard* and saw that he worked for Amazon, right?"

She checked the rearview mirror. Her pursuer's headlights were there, with a couple of cars in between them. She sighed. "Yeah."

"Okay, um..."

She heard Einstein typing.

"The real Bob Dennard lives in Salt Lake City," he said. "He's around the same age as the guy you met. Problem is, with only this picture, I can't figure out who's following you."

"Babe," Demon said, "you got the license plate for that car?"

Zahra kicked herself for not being as diligent as he was. "No."

"But he's still following you, right?"

"Yes, but he's a few cars behind. And it's dark. Shit, Demon. I'm sorry. I thought I did everything right."

"It's okay. Calm down. We'll figure this out. What kind of car is he in?"

"It's an Altima, dark red." She noticed the rattle in her voice. She squeezed her eyes closed for a moment and took a deep breath, forcing herself to remain calm.

"Where you at right now?" Demon asked. "What street?"

"I'm on University, headed, um, west."

"Okay, it's uh... Hold on a sec..."

She waited.

After a minute, Demon spoke again. "Alright, there's a Holiday Inn near you. I'ma text you the address, so you can put it in your GPS. I want you to go there. Einstein, make her a reservation, right quick." He gave him the address. "Baby, you got your Aida ID?"

Like the man following her, Zahra had several aliases, complete with phony driver's licenses. She didn't have to check her purse to know that she had the one he was inquiring about.

"Yes, I have it."

"You got that, Einstein? Make the reservation for *Aida Ferris.*"

He said, "I'm on it."

"When you get to the hotel," Demon said, "I want you to check in and let the people up front know that you might be followed."

She didn't think she'd heard him right. "Huh?"

"Tell 'em you got an ex-boyfriend who's been stalking you. Tell 'em to call you and let you know if he shows up. Give them the description of the guy you met."

He was starting to make sense now.

"Okay," she replied. "What do you want me to do after I check in, just wait there?"

"Yeah. For a little bit. I'ma put something in place to get you outta there, but it's gon' take a minute."

"Where are you? Are you still in Oklahoma?"

"Yes, but I can take care of this from here."

She had no doubt that he could. "Alright. You sent–" She received a notification on her phone. "Never mind. I got the address."

"Alright," Demon said. "Let me get off this phone so I can–"

"Wait." There was a break in the traffic behind her. She told him, "*I can see the license now.*"

"Okay, good. What is it?"

She stared at her rearview mirror and rattled off the information.

"You got that?" Demon asked Einstein.

"Yeah, I got it. Hold on a sec..."

They heard him typing again.

"Okay," Einstein said. "The car is registered to *Gerald Buchannan*. But the picture on *his* driver's license doesn't match the picture on the one that guy gave you. I'm sorry, Cleo. I still don't know who's following you. I gotta do more research. This car, I think is a good start."

"Damn." Zahra's eyes were wide, her mouth dry.

"It's gon' be alright," Demon told her. "I'ma get off this line so I can make some calls. Go ahead and make your way to that hotel. If I don't call you back before you check in, call me when you get to your room."

"Okay, baby. I'm sorry."

"It's okay. Don't worry. I'ma take care of this."

He disconnected.

∞ ∞ ∞ ∞ ∞ ∞ ∞

Zahra arrived at the hotel and checked in with no problem.

The clerk told her, "Wow, Miss Ferris. Someone *just* made this reservation, not even ten minutes ago. You must have been right down the street."

Zahra offered her a half smile. "Yeah. I was." After getting the keycard, she asked the woman, "Could you do me a favor?"

"Sure. What do you need?"

"I'm embarrassed to say this, but my ex-boyfriend has been following me around today. That's actually why I'm here. I'm trying to get a peaceful night's sleep. Could you tell me if someone comes here looking for me?"

Anxiety filled the woman's eyes. "I'm sorry to hear that. Do you want me to call the police? Are you in danger?"

"No, it's nothing like that," Zahra said. "He's not dangerous, just a little clingy. If you could give me a call if he shows up, that's all I need – oh, and don't tell him I'm here."

"No, Miss Ferris, we would never do that."

"Okay," Zahra said. "He's white, about six feet tall. He has blonde hair, blue eyes. Earlier today he was wearing khakis with a short-sleeved shirt."

"Okay..." The woman's concern had intensified.

"I'm sorry to put you in this position," Zahra said. "Don't worry. He won't cause any trouble."

"Yes, ma'am."

With that, Zahra left the desk and headed for the elevator. She took it up to the third floor and found her room. It was neat and cozy. It looked like a great place to spend the night, but she doubted if she'd be there that long. She crossed the room and pulled the blinds away from the windows. She didn't think the room overlooked the hotel's parking lot, and she was right.

She sighed and went to the bathroom. While staring at her reflection in the large mirror, she called Demon.

"You made it to the hotel?" he asked.

"Yes, I'm here. I told them to give me a call if someone came looking for me."

"Good. Did he follow you there?"

"He was still on my ass when I turned into the parking lot, but I didn't see him after that. He may have hung back a little. I doubt if he gave up that easily. Are you done with whatever you're doing to get me out of here?"

"Almost. I got some people in route, but—"

"Hold on a second," she told him. "Someone's calling me. Not too many people have this number..."

She accepted the other call. "Hello?"

"Hi, Miss Ferris?"

Her eyes widened. She could think of only one person who had this number *and* that alias. But the caller was male. "Yes."

"This is Bruce Jameson. I'm the manager here at the Holiday Inn."

"Oh, okay."

"My clerk tells me that you wanted to be notified if your boyfriend came here looking for you tonight. You told her that you did not want her to contact the police, but you thought he might be following you..."

"Yes, is something wrong?"

"Well, yes. A gentleman did come and inquire about you. He referred to you by a different name, but he described you, and the description you gave my clerk matches your ex-boyfriend. We did not tell him that you're here, and he left without causing any problems. However, the safety of our guests is my responsibility. I'm not sure why you don't want to get the police involved, but if this man returns, I have to let you know that we will contact the police."

Zahra played it cool. "Okay, if that's your policy, I understand. I didn't mean to cause any trouble."

"Miss Ferris, you haven't caused us any trouble. Melinda was shocked by how quickly he showed up after you checked in. You're right about him following you. We are concerned about you, and we want to do everything we can to help. We appreciate that you've chosen Holiday Inn to provide a safe haven in your time of need."

"Thank you."

She disconnected and returned to the other line.

"It was the front desk," she told Demon. "He just came in here looking for me."

"*That motherfucker*," Demon growled. "Alright. It's cool, baby. I just got a text from the team. They'll be ready in twenty minutes. In *exactly twenty minutes*, I want you to leave the hotel. When you get back on the road, call me, and I'll tell you which way to go."

"Who's coming? What are they gonna do?"

"We're still trying to figure that out. Just make sure you outta there when the time comes."

Zahra checked the time on her phone. It was 8:53 p.m. "Okay. I'll call you when I'm back on the road. Thank you. I love you."

"I love you too, baby. Talk to you later."

∞ ∞ ∞ ∞ ∞ ∞ ∞

Zahra had no idea what Demon put in place, but she trusted him fully. In exactly twenty minutes, she took the elevator down to the first floor. When she got to the lobby, the clerk who'd checked her in expressed curiosity and then alarm.

"Miss Ferris, are you leaving?"

"Yes," Zahra said. "Gonna go get something to eat."

"Are you sure that's a good idea? We have a restaurant here."

Zahra didn't want to be rude, but she had no idea how tight Demon's timeframe was. She'd already wasted precious time while waiting for the elevator.

"It's okay," she said without stopping. "I'll be back in a little bit."

She knew that might not be the case and felt guilty for lying to her. Melinda would probably be restless for the remainder of her shift, while waiting for Aida Ferris to return safely.

Zahra didn't spot the Altima in the hotel's parking lot, but it appeared behind her, once again a couple of cars back, once she made it to the main road. She called Demon.

He answered with, "You left?"

"Yes. He's following me again."

"Good."

She frowned at that. *Why was that good?*

"What street you on?" he asked.

"West 200th, headed east."

"Okay... Turn right on South Main, heading south."

"I just passed that street."

"Okay. Make the next right on South State and then turn right again on East Broadway. That'll take you back to South Main. When you get there, make a left."

As she followed the route, she asked him, "Why do you need me on South Main?"

"It's a nice, long street," he replied. "It'll give the team time to do what they need to do."

"And what is that?"

"A little something, something I cooked up. Let me know when you back on Main."

Zahra remained quiet until she reached the street he wanted. She then told him, "Okay, I'm on Main, headed south."

"Let me know when you get to Cesar Chavez. Should be coming up..."

When she got there, she told him, "Okay. I'm here."

"Bet. Keep driving like normal. I'll call you back." He disconnected.

Zahra checked her rearview mirror. After the turns, the man following her had lost the two-car buffer he started with. There was now only one car between her and the Altima. At the next intersection, she stopped for a red light.

She did not hear the motorcycles approaching, but she saw them in her rear and side mirrors. They swooped in like phantoms. There were four of them, all the same model. The riders wore helmets with the visors pulled down. As they neared the Altima, the first two bikes moved to the right and the left of the sedan, like water flowing around a rock. They came to a stop next to the driver and passenger doors. Zahra didn't realize there were two people on each bike until the passengers hopped off the back simultaneously. They too wore helmets that obscured their identities.

The passengers rushed to the Altima. Without a word, they smashed the front driver and passenger windows with what looked like metal Billy clubs. Just as quickly, they hopped back on the bikes, and the drivers took off. They sped past Zahra and ran the red light. She was so focused on the first two bikes, by the time she looked back again, the other two bikes had pulled up in the same positions as the first. Once again two passengers hopped off. Rather than clubs, they toted what looked like bottles. They ignited a rag hanging from the top of the incendiaries and threw them into the broken windows of the Altima. The cabin of the sedan erupted in flames.

Zahra's eyes grew large as she watched them.

Holy shit.

A little something, something I cooked up.

The bikers hopped back on the bikes, and the drivers sped away. They swooped past Zahra, ran the red light, and disappeared into the night.

The light turned green.

Zahra was so caught up in the scene behind her, she didn't immediately realize that the time to flee the scene was upon her. She couldn't tell if the man in the Altima was trying to get out of the car. All she saw was fire. It billowed out of the busted windows. Even if a fire truck was already on the scene, it was unlikely they could have saved the man who had told her his name was Bob Dennard.

Zahra removed her foot from the brake and calmly drove through the intersection, as if she had nothing to do with the dramatic murder that had just occurred.

CHAPTER TEN
TINDERBOX

From the crime scene, Zahra headed to the tactical point in the same city. Once there, she had the opportunity to meet some of the bikers who had come to her rescue. A couple of them were women. Another two were new recruits. The question of whether these white soldiers were loyal had never been an issue for her, especially after seeing Hulk in action. But after tonight, she trusted Demon's judgment even more. She thanked them, and they spent the next few hours monitoring the news of the murder as it trickled into the media outlets.

The mission had been a success, which was no surprise to Zahra. She knew there was no way the occupant of the Altima could survive. A reporter interviewed a homicide detective who said the murder had the hallmark of a gang killing, but it was too early in the investigation to know for sure. They had no suspects. Witnesses indicated three or four motorcycles were involved. At this time, the identity of the victim was unknown, and given the condition of the body, the detective declined to offer a timeline on when an identification may be possible.

The next morning, Zahra caught a flight to Texas. Demon was waiting for her at their Houston headquarters. He rarely offered more than a hug when they were around others. Today was no different, but his caress told the story of how much she meant to him. He held her tightly in his strong arms as if they hadn't seen each other in years. The previous evening, he seemed more upset with the man following her than genuinely concerned about her safety. His embrace spoke volumes about how worried he had been.

He took her bag and told her, "I'ma take this upstairs. I'll meet you in the computer room when I'm done."

"Okay."

When she got to the room, she saw that the group's top brass was there. Head and Einstein greeted her cordially.

Cujo gave a perfunctory, "What's up," but offered no smile.

This was his custom, at least when it came to her, so she didn't bother asking him what was wrong.

"Check this out," Einstein said.

Zahra stepped closer to him. On his computer, she saw a picture of the man she had attempted to recruit last night. Her heart skipped a beat, as memories of the fire flooded her.

"His real name is *Donald Herring*. He was an investigative reporter for the Wall Street Journal."

Studying his screen, Zahra saw that Einstein was on the publication's website. Herring had an extensive bio.

"He's traveled to wars," Einstein stated, "done a lot of political stuff. He did a big exposé on right wing militias a few years back. Won a Pulitzer for that."

Zahra's sense of dread deepened. They'd murdered a Pulitzer Prize recipient – at Demon's behest.

They did that for her.

"The police haven't identified him," Einstein went on. "I figured out who he was by tracking the Altima. The guy it's registered to is also a reporter. It won't be long before the police put it all together, but they'll need dental records for a positive ID; that guy is burnt to a crisp."

Zahra nodded, saying nothing.

Demon joined them at that moment.

Cujo looked his way and said, "We need to talk."

"That's cool," Demon replied. He stepped further into the room and took a seat on the futon next to Zahra. "What's up?"

"Not here," Cujo said. "Let's do this privately."

Demon shook his head. "Naw, man. I ain't doing that no more. From now on, anything you got to say to me, you can say it in front of these people."

Cujo's demeanor darkened. "Okay. I'm cool with Head and Einstein, but you including Cleo in our core now?"

"No, but I'm pretty sure whatever you wanna talk about has something to do with her, so you should say it while she's here."

Cujo shot Zahra a look that was so venomous, she could taste the poison.

"Fine," he said. "I think that what y'all did last night was *reckless*, and once again you've endangered our whole organization."

"What I did last night was save a member of our organization. How you figure it was reckless? I put a lot of thought into that killing. That's why we torched the car instead of shooting it up. If the guy had been doing surveillance on us, I wanted to make sure we destroyed whatever evidence he had on him."

"It's reckless because you didn't know who that man was when you made that call. He could've been a federal agent."

"That wouldn't have changed anything," Demon said coldly.

Cujo's eyes widened. "So, you moving the goal post again? We never killed a cop before."

"And we still haven't."

"You said you were willing to."

"I was willing to do whatever was necessary to get one of our people out of danger. I would've done the same if it was you."

"I appreciate you saying that, but I think that if you're going to do something like that, more people should be involved in the decision. But as usual, you're willing to drag us down whatever path you want, as if your opinion is the only one that matters."

The other three people in the room watched the back and forth anxiously, like children in the uncomfortable position of watching their parents argue.

"And to be honest, I don't think you would've done that if it was me being followed," Cujo stated. "I think you only did that because it was *Cleo*, and you were thinking with your *dick* instead of your brain."

Zahra could take no more of this. "I think you don't know what you're talking about. Demon is always there for all of us. He does so much for this group. All you do is complain."

"Did you hear me talking to you?" Cujo snapped back.

"Don't talk to her like that," Demon warned.

Cujo held his ground. "Or what? Is that a threat? I told you I wanted to talk to you privately. You allowed her to be part of this meeting, and now you gonna let her run her mouth when she has no idea what she's talking about?" To Zahra, he said, "The fact that you had a place to lay your head last night is because of *me*. Do you think all those tactical points, safehouses – all those cars in the storage units with weapons in the trunk just magically appear?"

Zahra's nostrils flared. She didn't respond.

"Cujo does a lot for our group," Demon told his woman. "But you do a lot of complaining too," he said to Cujo.

"Offering a voice of reason ain't complaining," Cujo emphasized. "I meant what I said: You shouldn't make a decision to kill someone *who might be a cop* without talking to me first."

"But it wasn't a cop."

"*You didn't know that at the time*! Plus, this man was *innocent*. He was a reporter doing his damn job. He never harmed anyone in our group. You should've waited for Einstein to figure out who he was before you started making calls. You got eight of our people wrapped up in this. I won't even ask if you gave them an option. I'm sure you just told them what to do, and they did it because the order came from you!"

Demon nodded. He was fuming, but he surprised everyone by saying, "Okay. You right. I should've waited. But we all know hindsight is 20/20."

Cujo kept his foot on the gas, rather than accept the concession. "Are you willing to admit that your emotions played a part in your decision – because it was *her*?"

The way he spat the pronoun out, Zahra thought he might as well replace it with *that bitch*.

Demon shook his head. "No. I told you I would've done the same for you. I meant that."

"Whatever," Cujo said. He turned and left the room.

After several moments of silence, Head said, "Well, that was awkward."

"I feel you," Demon said. He rose to his feet with a sigh. "You ready to go up, babe? I know you tired."

Zahra was more frustrated than tired, but she stood as well. "Yeah. I'm ready."

They left the room together and headed upstairs.

∞ ∞ ∞ ∞ ∞ ∞ ∞

When they were alone, Zahra took a shower and left the bathroom wearing a robe. She headed for the closet to find an outfit for the day, but Demon called her to the bed, where he was sitting, working on his laptop. He placed the device aside when she sat next to him. He watched her for a moment and reached to brush the hair away from her eyes.

He asked her, "What's wrong?"

In addition to weariness, her anxiety was palpable. She sighed and told him, "I don't like how things are going. I'm sorry for what I said to Cujo. I know I was wrong."

"You weren't wrong for speaking up. You have a right to say how you feel."

"I know. But I shouldn't have said that he doesn't do anything but complain. It's just... I get so frustrated with the way he talks to you. I should've kept my mouth shut, though. It wasn't my place to defend you. It only made things worse."

"That argument was going down regardless of whether you got involved or not. You are never wrong to stick up for me. You know I would do the same for you."

She looked into his eyes and nibbled on her bottom lip.

He asked her, "What else is bothering you?"

She shook her head, her expression downcast. "It's a lot going on, David. We're doing so much."

"You think we're doing *too* much?"

"I don't know. I feel bad about that reporter. I didn't like the way he was following me, but Cujo's right. He was just doing his job. I don't like it when innocent people get hurt."

"You feel the same way about the women at that club?"

"No. They were aligned with that Aryan gang. If they think it's cool to go out with people like that, they don't get a pass when their boyfriends get what's coming to 'em."

"What about the boy Tasha and Zulu killed?"

She continued to shake her head. "No. He was young, but he was armed. I agree with you about what kind of person he was gonna turn out to be."

"So, as far as innocents, it's just this reporter that you're upset about?"

"Yeah. That man, he was so successful. And the exposé he did on right-wing militias, that shows that he's not one-sided. He went after them the same way he went after us. All he wanted to do was write a good story. You know the blowback for this is gonna be bad. When people find out what he was doing when he got killed, they'll hate us even more."

Demon took all of that in and said, "Zahra, that's the way our group is set up. They always gon' hate us. But like Head was saying the other day, there are a lot of people who support what we're doing. Personally, I don't care how the world views us, as long as we accomplish our goals. Don't forget that white people been hating us for centuries. They been killing us for no reason at all. They don't have the moral standing to get mad now that we starting to get even."

She nodded. "You're right. But I can't help but feel guilty about the part I played in this reporter situation, how I messed up with recruiting. If I had done a good job vetting him, he never would've got that close to us."

"You don't know that. You said so yourself, he was very good at what he does. I understand why you feel guilty, but the way I see it, everything we do is about sending a message. What we did last night was a very strong message. Do you think another reporter will be so quick to do an investigative piece on us? Hell naw.

We put out the word that if *anybody* comes for us, whether it be the police, a white supremacist or a damn reporter, we'll take counteractions to put down the threat. The moment we start showing weakness will be the moment all our asses end up on death row."

She nodded, appreciating the time he took to counsel and mentor her.

He smiled. "What happened to that bad bitch who got about forty bodies under her belt? I like your sensitive side, but where that other chick at?"

"*Forty?*" she said chuckling. "I don't have forty bodies."

"Damn if you don't. What was it, fourteen at the club. Nine in them woods. And that's just the recent shit. Sheee, I think you prolly up to more like fifty or sixty."

"*Damn*," Zahra said, doing the math. "You prolly right. That's crazy, I killed all those people." Her eyes brightened. "David, I really have killed *fifty or sixty people*. Shit, what does it say about me if I done lost count?"

He laughed at that. "While you're thinking about that, think about how many black lives you saved or avenged so far. How a bad-ass assassin like you let somebody like *Cujo* get in yo head?"

"Cujo is pretty important. He's a founder of this group."

"Cujo ain't got a gun in his hand every night." Demon stood and positioned himself in front of her. He reached and pulled her robe open, revealing her succulent nude flesh. "And he ain't the one in here about to eat this pussy," he continued.

An instant rush of heat made her skin sizzle.

"Umm, neither are you," she told him.

"Damn if I ain't." He guided her shoulders back on the bed, until she lie flat with her feet dangling over the edge.

Staring at the ceiling, she told him, "David, it's the middle of the day. People are here."

"Yo pussy taste the best in the middle of the day, when people are here." He dropped to his knees and raised her legs over his shoulders.

Before he wrapped his lips around her clit, she told him, "When I was in Detroit, I took care of what we were talking about."

He looked up at her. "We talked about a lot of things..."

"The birth control."

"No shit?"

Her face flushed as she nodded. "Yes."

"How long ago was that?"

She propped herself on her elbows so she could see his face. The sight of his eyes peering over her mound made her legs tremble.

"It's been eight days," she told him. "The doctor said I had to wait seven before we could go without a condom."

From that vantage point, she couldn't see his mouth, but she felt his breath on her labia.

His eyes remained locked on hers as he licked her slowly and soundly. Between licks he said, "That mean I can raw dog this pussy after I get through eating it?..."

This was too much. The sight, the sensations, his dirty talk. She could not understand why Demon's aggressive side was such a turn on.

"Yes." She lie back and closed her eyes. "I been dying to feel you cum inside me."

Demon quieted down and used his lips, tongue and fingers to reward her beauty and her loyalty. By the time he came up for air, his face glistened from the nose down. He told her to scoot further onto the bed, as he quickly shed his clothes. He crawled on top of her and took his time with the insertion. He rubbed the tip of his bare dick between her labia and over her clitoris for a few pleasing seconds.

"I been waiting so long to feel this," he breathed. "I'm sorry, but I'm prolly gon' cum in a couple of minutes."

Zahra was too numb to respond.

She gasped when he pushed all the way in. Her eyes fluttered open. They were face to face. His eyes were as dark and dreamy as she felt. She reached for his head and pulled him closer. She sucked her essence off his lips as he slowly grinded in her box.

He was right. No one mattered but him. All that he was. All that they were.

CHAPTER ELEVEN
BLOODY MESS

Demon and Zahra spent the whole day together at the Houston Headquarters. Cujo left the house after their morning meeting, so they didn't have to contend with his ominous presence. Demon made salmon and rice for lunch. While they ate, they kept up with news about the reporter's murder as more information became available. The world now knew that the victim was a journalist for the Wall Street Journal, and he had been working on a story about the Ace of Spades at the time of his death. Detectives did not definitively assert that the group was responsible for his murder, but they believed this was the most likely conclusion.

"If so," a reporter noted, "this would mark yet another dark turning point for this group, which is allegedly responsible for hundreds of deaths across the country. MSNBC stands with all journalists. Our thoughts and prayers are with Mr. Herring's family as they cope with this unspeakable tragedy."

Demon didn't think it was a good idea for Zahra to watch the memorial reels some news agencies had hastily put together to celebrate the journalist's legacy. She watched them anyway. Whenever she participated in a mission, she did her research on the targets. She didn't think this one should be any different, even if it was after the fact.

The next morning, Demon got dressed and packed a bag for another flight. Zahra did the same.

Before leaving, he asked her, "Are you sure you're ready to get back into it? I can get somebody else to work with Simone today. I got people in the area."

"It's okay," she replied. "We already had this planned. I wanna go."

"Baby, you know I appreciate your work ethic. But it's okay to take a break. You been stressed out. I think you should chill for another day or two."

"If I do that, I won't do nothing but watch news about that reporter. I'll probably get in my feelings again, especially if you're not here. It's better for me to stay busy. I wanna work."

"Okay." He stepped closer and gave her a hug and a soft kiss. "Y'all be careful."

"We will. Happy hunting."

He smiled at that. "Same to you."

∞ ∞ ∞ ∞ ∞ ∞ ∞

Four hours later, she was back in the Sunshine State. This time her plane touched down in Miami. She took a rental to a storage unit (thinking of Cujo as she did so) and swapped it with a Charger he had stashed here. She had a little time on her hands, so she stopped by CJ's Crab Shack for lunch. The food was excellent. Zahra regretted her decision not to wait for her partner when Simone called towards the end of the meal.

"Just got my rental from the airport," Simone informed her. "Where you be?"

"I stopped at a crab shack for lunch. Headed to the tactical point when I leave here."

"Bitch, you eating without me? *Trifling*."

Laughing, Zahra told her, "I would've waited, but I wasn't sure about your ETA. You want me to get something for you before I leave? The food here is really good."

"Girl, don't nobody want no *cold crab*. It won't taste as good coming out the microwave."

"Yeah, that's true."

"Guess I'll stop at McDonalds. It's gon' be time to get moving, by the time I make it to the tac point."

"McDonalds is just as good. The food here ain't all that."

"Lies! That's alright, though. I'll see you in a little bit."

∞ ∞ ∞ ∞ ∞ ∞ ∞

An hour and a half later, night had fallen. The women sat in the parking lot of the Lowes Home Improvement store in Hialeah. Simone was behind the wheel of the Charger. They weren't sure which one of the store's exits the daytime manager would use at the end of his shift, so they kept their eyes on both. While waiting, they strategized their plan of attack. Compared to the last time they were together, tonight's mission would be more straight forward.

They didn't expect to have to contend with an innocent bystander, and they both agreed the target should have the opportunity to speak before they sealed his fate. There was nothing he could say that would change what was about to happen to him, but his incident made national news a few years ago. The assassins were aware of what he'd told the jury. They wanted to hear it for themselves.

At 10:24 p.m., Richard Vessels emerged from the store still wearing his bright red work vest. His killers knew which vehicle he would head to in the parking lot. Simone started their car as he climbed into his truck. She gave him a little leeway when he exited the parking lot and allowed a few cars to get between them when they got to the main road. They knew where he was going. There was no worry that they might lose him during the fifteen-minute drive.

In addition to being a murderer, Vessels was an adulterer. According to his phone records, he texted his mistress throughout the day while at work. He sometimes texted during the drive home. Upon arriving at his residence, he had a habit of sending one last text before going inside to his wife. It was this last text that would be his undoing. Vessels composed this message after he pulled into his driveway and turned his car off. A surveillance team had discovered that he never closed his garage from inside his car. Instead, he exited his truck and used the button mounted to the left of the back door.

While writing his last message on this night, Vessels was fully focused on the sultry emotions he hoped to conjure. With his head in the clouds and his garage door open, his killers crept from around the side of the house and rushed into the garage. By the time Vessels realized something was amiss, they had taken positions on both sides of his truck. The intruders wore ski masks. They were both armed. Simone had the barrel of her weapon against the driver's side window. Zahra's gun was aimed at the passenger window.

At that point, Vessels was as good as dead. The only unknown was whether he would comply with the one task they needed from him.

"Unlock the door," Simone said. Her voice was stern and assertive. "You ain't gotta die tonight, but you can if you want to."

Vessels' hands were frozen in place on his phone. His chest began to rise and fall visibly. He first stared at

Simone, and then whipped his head to the right and studied Zahra. She nodded but said nothing.

Simone spoke again, loud enough to be heard through the window, but hopefully not loudly enough for the lone occupant of the house to hear.

"Don't be stupid. Yo phone and whatever money you got in yo wallet ain't worth yo life. Unlock the door, give us what we after, and we'll be on our way. If you don't, I'ma shoot you through this window and still take yo shit. We can go that route if you want. It's up to you..."

Zahra had to fight to keep from smiling when Vessels reached to unlock the doors. In the back of her mind, she heard Redd Foxx admonishing his TV son.

You big dummy!

As soon as they heard the locks disengage, they sprang into action. Zahra yanked the door open and hopped into the passenger seat. Simone climbed into the backseat of the quad cab. Simone swapped her pistol for a combat knife, which she used to poke Vessels in the side of the neck. Zahra kept her gun trained on his midsection.

"*Goddammit, I knew it was you!*" Vessels said, panting now.

He reached for his car horn. Zahra blocked him with her free hand.

"*If you hit that horn, you gon' die,*" she growled.

"*You gonna kill me anyway. This isn't a robbery.*"

Vessels was in his mid-forties. He had dark hair and was clean-shaven. He was chubby but had not graduated to fat.

"You right," Zahra said. "You know who we are, and you know we're gonna leave an ace of spades in this truck when we're done with you. The only question is whether or not we go in your house and do the same to your wife."

"Fuck that," Simone breathed. "If you hit that horn, I'ma make sure yo wife die slow. She'll curse you before it's all said and done. You feel this thang on yo neck? This blade is *8 inches long*. This my *Rambo knife*. It's so sharp, I can shove it all the way through your throat. I'll gut yo woman with this knife, if I have to. I'll gut her and let her bleed out."

Still breathing roughly, Vessels considered his options for much longer than Zahra was comfortable with before he lowered his hands.

"Good," she said. "Is your wife sleep?"

"Huh, huh?"

"I need to know how much time we have," she said. "Is she gonna come out and check on you?"

He shook his head. "No. I – I usually wake her up when I get home."

"Good," Simone said. "Now all that's left is for you to answer a few questions, starting with *Why'd you kill Draymond*? And don't gimme that shit you was saying in court. That boy wasn't nothing but fourteen. It didn't have to come to that."

169

Tears spilled from the man's eyes. *"I told the truth. He attacked me. He hit me first."*

"You were in your house minding your business," Zahra reminded him. "Draymond was at a house party down the street. Two neighbors called the police to complain about the noise. That was a bitch move too, but that type of shit is expected. You could've made the same call. Instead, you grabbed your gun and marched your happy-ass down there like you the fucking sheriff."

"What'd you take the gun for?" Simone snapped.

"I – I always carry it."

"Bullshit. The prosecutor said you could see through your window that your white neighbor had some black kids at his party. That's why you took your gun, ain't it?"

"No. I swear!"

"What difference does it make at this point," Zahra said. "Why lie? You gon' die either way. We just want the truth."

His head slumped in defeat. Snot now joined the tears streaming down his face. "I'm not gonna say I did that because he was black. That's not why. I asked them to turn the music down, and they got aggressive. I was outnumbered. Draymond hit me first. I had a right to defend myself."

Zahra knew they wouldn't get the desired response from this man. He understood Florida's Stand Your Ground law. In court, the jury had no choice but to acquit him, even though he admitted to instigating the altercation that led to an unarmed black teen being shot dead.

She switched gears and asked, "Why'd you embrace the white nationalists afterwards?"

"*I didn't!*"

"Liar. You became their poster child. You spoke at their rallies. I got receipts."

"They embraced me, but, but I never said I was one of them."

"They paid you?" Simone asked from the back seat.

"Huh?"

"Did they pay you?" she asked again, hammering each word. "Have you received upwards of two hundred thousand dollars from white nationalist groups that raised money for you?"

"*That was for my trial,*" he cried.

"So, you don't support them, but you're okay with them supporting you and paying for your trial?" Zahra asked. "You spoke at their events as a way of saying thank you?"

Vessels' eyes darted. He knew there was no escape, but he had not relinquished the will to live.

"The money didn't even go to your trial," Simone said. "Your lawyer took that case pro bono. Getting you off got him a lot of publicity. We might have to go see his ass later."

"What'd you do with the money?" Zahra asked.

Simone didn't give him a chance to respond. "Spent fifty-three thousand on a pool. That's one thing you did."

"And you paid for this brand-new truck – with cash," Zahra said.

Simone said, "So, you kill poor, little Draymond and get rewarded with a truck, a pool, and a nice cushion in your savings account. Funny how things work out, ain't it?"

"My last question," Zahra said, "is why haven't you ever apologized for what you did? I get that you wanted to beat the case, but you could'a said, '*I'm sorry I killed that child, but I was defending myself.*' That wouldn't have messed up your acquittal."

Vessels raised his head. Tears continued to stream down his cheeks. He was nearly blubbering when he managed to say something Draymond's mother had wanted to hear for the past three years.

"*I, I'm sorry.*"

"Yeah, and I'm sorry that I still have to kill your wife," Simone said.

Vessels' eyes flashed open. "Huh?"

Before he could look back at her, she slammed the knife into the side of his neck. She didn't have enough momentum to shove the blade all the way to the hilt, but she got half of it in. Zahra registered shock as the lethal wound sprayed her with blood. She felt it soaking her ski mask. It was in her eyes, on her mouth. Simone removed the blade (which made more blood squirt) and stabbed him again, and again. All of these blows were on his right side. Zahra was the unwilling recipient of the messy aftermath.

Vessels first reached for his throat. He barely noticed when one of his fingers was nearly severed. He thrashed out with his legs. Simone was up to six stabs by then. Seven. Eight. With his last bit of strength, Vessels reached for the car horn. Zahra barely saw the move through the blood in her eyes. She dropped her gun and scrambled to block his hands. She fought with him for what felt like an eternity before his movements gradually ceased, and he slumped in his seat. Gravity pulled his dying body in Zahra's direction. She had to fight again, shoving with all of her might to keep him out of her lap.

She reached for her door handle and was able to squeeze out of the truck. She was drenched with blood. She was pissed. She had so much DNA on her, their getaway was now complicated. Simone tossed a playing card onto the front seat before exiting on her side. She and Zahra met at the back of the vehicle. Despite her anger and the rush of adrenaline that had her heart doing double time, Zahra kept her voice at a hush when she confronted her partner.

"*Damn, bitch! Why you do that?*"

"I'm sorry," Simone said, in the same quiet tone. "I lost my cool."

"*Damn right, you lost your cool*! How I'm supposed to ride all the way back to the tactical point looking like this?"

"Just get in the backseat and lie down," Simone advised her. "I'll take the back roads. We'll be fine. Where yo gun?"

Zahra nearly slipped on the blood coating the garage's concrete floor as she returned to the truck to retrieve her pistol.

One minute later, the ladies were back in the Charger.

Zahra simmered in the back seat as Simone put the car in drive and fled the scene.

CHAPTER TWELVE
TRUST ISSUES

Zahra didn't think she'd ever taken a longer and hotter shower. She had to wash her hair three times before the water that drained down the tub no longer had traces of blood. She knew they'd have to torch the getaway car. No deep cleaning could remove all traces of Vessels' DNA from the backseat.

She was no longer upset with Simone when she stepped out of the bathtub, but she planned to tell Demon that she did not want to work with her again. In their line of work, it was understandable to get emotional from time to time. Zahra had experienced that herself in the past few days. But she would never allow her emotions to reach a boiling point during a mission. What Simone had done was unacceptable.

She left the bathroom wearing a robe over her camisole and panties. Before heading to bed, she stopped by the kitchen and found Simone standing at the counter. It was just the two of them in the house that night.

"You hungry?" Simone asked.

Zahra shook her head but asked, "Did they leave anything good?"

Simone crossed the room and opened the refrigerator. Zahra didn't know who was responsible for making sure there were rations available at their safehouses, but there was always something there for hungry soldiers.

"I don't know how long this ham has been in here," Simone said, looking through the fridge. "But it hasn't expired yet. The bread is still good." She closed the door and checked the freezer. "We got plenty frozen dinners. I don't know if I would eat this *meatloaf*," she said, shifting through the boxes. "This Salisbury steak don't look half bad."

"I had a big lunch," Zahra said. "I'm good."

"I did find this," Simone said, returning to the counter. She hefted a bottle of champagne. Zahra noticed that she'd already poured a glass for both of them. "Here. Let's celebrate." She offered her one of the glasses.

Zahra approached the counter but shook her head. "Nah. I'm good. I'm too tired. That'll put me straight to sleep."

"What's wrong with that?" Simone asked, smiling. "I think we both need a good night's sleep, after what we been through."

Zahra returned the smile but shook her head. "Uh uhn. I haven't eaten anything since lunch. I'm not hungry, but don't like drinking on an empty stomach."

"You don't celebrate after your missions?"

"I do, sometimes."

"You don't want to tonight?"

"It's not that. I told you; I don't like to drink on an empty stomach."

"I can make you something to eat."

Zahra continued to shake her head.

"You mad at me about what happened, right?" Simone guessed. "That's why you don't wanna celebrate with me..."

"Um, I ain't gon' lie. I was irritated. But that's not it."

"Then what's the problem?"

Zahra chuckled. "Fine." She took the glass. "Damn. I don't think I ever experienced peer pressure like this."

Simone laughed. "If it wasn't for peer pressure, wouldn't nobody ever have no fun."

Zahra brought the glass to her lips, and her stomach churned uncomfortably. Even Simone heard it.

She said, "Damn, girl. Is that your stomach?"

"Yeah," Zahra said. "I told you I haven't eaten in a while. I don't think I should put alcohol on top of whatever's going on in there."

"Let me get you something to eat," Simone said, returning to the refrigerator. "Do you want a sandwich, or one of these frozen dinners?"

Zahra gave her a look and said, "A sandwich, I guess. I can make it, though."

"That's alright, girl. I got you. I owe you for getting all that blood on you."

Zahra took her glass to the kitchen table and took a seat. She watched her friend take items from the fridge to make the sandwich. When Simone stepped out of view in search of a paper plate, Zahra opened her robe and poured her drink on her chest. She cringed at the cold sensation as the liquor soaked her camisole and flowed down between her legs. She closed her robe and placed the empty glass on the table.

Simone headed her way two minutes later with the plate in hand. She noticed the empty glass and said, "You drank that already?"

"Yeah," Zahra said. She forced a smile. "It was good. Sorry, was I supposed to wait on you?"

"*I guess not*," Simone said, chuckling. She placed the sandwich before her. "You want another drink?"

Zahra shook her head. "No. I prolly shouldn't have had that one."

Simone returned to the kitchen and retrieved her own glass. In the interim, Zahra stared at the sandwich. She had misgivings about it too. She lifted the top bread but didn't see anything amiss. Simone saw her checking it when she returned.

"What's wrong?"

"Wanted to see if it had some cheese."

"We don't have any."

"That's okay," Zahra said. "It still looks good."

They didn't speak much while she ate the sandwich, and Simone drank her champagne. By the time they were done, a good deal of moisture had settled around Zahra's butt. She hoped the bottom of her dark-colored robe would absorb the liquid. She stood and casually checked the seat of her chair. There was a bit of champagne on it, but not too much. Zahra pushed the chair under the table.

"I'm tired," she said. That was true, but she exaggerated her look of fatigue. "I'ma take my ass to bed."

Simone watched her. "Okay."

As she left the room, Zahra staggered slightly and used the doorframe to support herself. "Whoa." She looked back at Simone to see how she'd react to that.

Simone continued to study her. Her smile was gone now. Zahra didn't want to think there was *cunning* in her eyes, but she could think of no other way to describe it.

"You okay?" Simone asked.

"Yeah," Zahra said. Her voice sounded as groggy as she appeared. "Champagne on an empty stomach – not a good idea. I hope the sandwich helps."

"I'm sure it will," Simone said. "You better go lay down."

"Yeah," Zahra said. "I'll see you in the morning."

∞ ∞ ∞ ∞ ∞ ∞ ∞

She was not asleep when Simone came to check on her. She wasn't sure how much time had passed, but she was wide awake. Alert. Waiting. Her eyes, however, were mostly closed. Zahra could barely see through the slits, but she forced herself not to open them wider. She was lying on her side facing the door. Her heart froze when Simone slowly opened it.

"Hey," Simone said. "You awake?"

Zahra did not respond.

Simone spoke louder. "Cleo. You sleep?"

No response.

Zahra watched her friend do something she'd seen before. Simone had a small bottle in one hand, a cloth in the other. She squirted the contents of the bottle onto the cloth and tucked the bottle in her back pocket. She then made her way into the room.

Zahra remained completely still.

She thought about the champagne, how insistent Simone was about her drinking it.

I'm good with chemicals.

A part of her couldn't believe this was happening, but her eyes were not deceiving her. This seemed like a severe overreaction to the way Zahra had snapped at her after their mission. She had called Simone a bitch, but they moved past that. Zahra suspected Simone had put something in her glass to put her to sleep, but what was she doing now? There was no point in drugging her twice, unless there was something different in the bottle, different than what Simone had used on Bearfield's daughter.

Prolly could'a been an anesthesiologist, if life hadn't led me down this other road.

When she was within a few feet of the bed, Zahra opened her eyes. She pulled the sheets back with her free hand, revealing a silenced pistol in the other. The gun was pointed at Simone.

A few seconds of silence passed before Zahra asked her, "What are you doing?"

Stunned, Simone could not articulate a response. She had concealed the hand holding the cloth behind her back.

Zahra sat up. Her heart thundered, but her voice was calm. "What are you doing?" she asked again.

Simone took a step back.

Zahra told her, "Don't move."

Simone took a deep breath and another step back. Zahra didn't think she was armed, but there were plenty of guns in the house. If she let her make it out of the room, they'd have a shootout at the O.K. Corral.

She warned her once more. "Simone, don't take another step."

Simone finally spoke. "It's not what you think." She took another step back. She was near the doorway now.

THUMP!

The silenced report sounded enormous in the quiet house. The gun bucked in Zahra's hand. Simone's mouth fell open as a bright, red stain blossomed on her white shirt. She stumbled backwards and then fell to her butt. By the time Zahra made it out of the bed, Simone was flat on her back. The hole in her chest bled profusely.

Gasping, she said, "*He, hel, help. Help. Ca, call help. Please. Please. Help.*" Simone reached for her wound with fingers that were stiff and twisted.

Zahra knelt next to her. Tears filled her eyes. "Why you do this? Why you make me do this?"

"*Doing...*" Simone swallowed. "*Doing, doing too much. You – you and Demon. Too much... Please, call, call... Help.*"

Demon? Zahra's brain raced. What did Demon have to do with this?

"*Please...*"

Simone was bleeding from the mouth now. Zahra knew that even if she made the call, help would not arrive in time.

But she had no intention of making the call.

As she watched her friend die, she accepted the actuality that they were never really friends. That small tweak in her perception made this crisis a little easier to deal with.

∞ ∞ ∞ ∞ ∞ ∞ ∞

In retrospect, Demon should've known something was up. After spending the day in Boston surveilling a target, he drove four hours to get to a tactical point they'd established in New York. He was dead tired when he finally arrived at 11 p.m. He was surprised to see another car in the garage. He knew there was no other team working in the area that night.

Inside the safehouse, his confusion deepened when he encountered Cujo in the kitchen. Cujo was a consummate family guy. He traveled across the country to set up the tactical points and storage units for the group, but he rarely spent the night outside of his wife's bed.

"Hey, man. What's up?" Demon toted a duffle bag that was filled with a variety of armaments that may be necessary for his next mission. He deposited the bag on the floor next to the door.

"What's up," Cujo replied. "I was in the area stocking up on supplies. Thought I'd bring some by here."

"You been in the city all day?" Demon asked.

"I been on this coast," Cujo said. "This is my last stop."

"Oh." Demon nodded. "What kind of supplies?"

"Boring shit," he said with a chuckle. "Groceries, toilet paper, soap, shampoo."

"May be boring, but that stuff's essential," Demon replied. "I appreciate you for keeping up with that." He

183

checked his watch. "It's pretty late. You catching a red eye or..."

"I figured I'd crash here tonight and dip out in the morning," Cujo stated, "if that's alright with you."

Demon shrugged. "It's cool with me. What groceries did you bring?" He looked past him and noticed a pizza box on the kitchen island. "Tell me it's still some pizza in there."

"The whole pizza is there," Cujo said, grinning. "I haven't ate yet."

He flipped the box open, and Demon saw that he'd brought a meat lovers.

"That's my favorite."

"Yeah, I know," Cujo said. "I remember them late night meetings we used to have back in the day. You was always willing to stay up however long it took to figure things out, as long as we ordered one of these. And I got this too..." He turned and grabbed a bottle of D'ussé off the counter. "I thought we'd have a few sips, for old times sake."

Demon's look of confusion returned. "You knew I was gon' be here?"

The larger man nodded. "Yeah. Einstein told me." When Demon continued to stare at him, Cujo said, "Look, I know we had a lot of disagreements lately. But you and I both know that ain't good for the group. I blame you most of the time, but the truth is, our problems are as much my fault as yours. I was hoping we could break bread and move past all the bullshit. We need to move on, if that's okay with you..."

Demon knew he could be an asshole at times, but he wasn't a big enough asshole to tell Cujo to go to hell when he was trying to be the bigger man. Besides, Cujo was right. They had to get past their differences and do what was best for the group.

"I'm cool with that." He stepped to him and dapped him up. "Where the plates at?" he asked, looking down at the pizza. "I'm ready to tear this shit up."

∞ ∞ ∞ ∞ ∞ ∞ ∞

Demon could barely recall eating the pizza or enjoying the two drinks Cujo served him. What he did remember was how tired he was towards the end of the meal. He was already exhausted when he arrived at the safe house, but what he felt after spending time with Cujo went far beyond any fatigue he'd ever experienced. It was as if he'd been awakened in the wee hours of the morning and was struggling to get his wits about him.

He remembered telling Cujo that he was sleepy. He remembered how Cujo remained seated at the kitchen island when he stood and headed for the bedroom. He remembered glancing at the duffle bag he'd brought inside with him. He planned to take it to the room with him, but the act of crossing the kitchen and bending to retrieve it was too much effort. That struck him as odd, because a task so simple shouldn't seem as daunting as digging a ditch. But that's the way he felt about it.

Man, fuck that bag.

Another thing he found peculiar was his unwillingness to bathe that night. During the drive from Boston, he'd been looking forward to how good the shower would feel when he got to the tactical point. But when he made it to the bedroom, taking off his clothes and standing under the spray of water was the *last* thing he wanted to do. That was a bridge too far.

Man, fuck a shower.

The only thing he truly wanted was to sleep. He felt like he could sleep for a hundred years. He felt like he *needed* to sleep for that long.

Demon had never been drugged before. He always assumed that if something like that ever happened to him, he would be aware of it. He thought that as he neared a state of unconsciousness, he would feel panicked and wonder what was wrong with him. But it was nothing like that. There were a few parts of the experience that felt a little off, like not wanting to pick up the duffle bag or take a shower. But for the most part, the need to close his eyes felt completely natural, as the need to rest was a normal part of any other night.

He wasn't sure if he ever made it to the bed.

Sleep was pleasant, until it wasn't.

He dreamt about a monster. With red eyes, teeth bared, spittle glistening on its lips. It was a big, dark monster that made no sound as it wrapped its claws around his throat and began to choke him. In the midst of the dream, Demon did not panic, even though this was the most real and terrifying dream he'd ever experienced. He felt the monster's weight on him. The claws clamped around his neck, squeezing the life out of him, felt very real. In his dream, Demon could not breathe. He'd had nightmares before, but he never lost the ability to *breathe* in a dream. He never felt his chest burn and his eyes bulge like this.

If this night had proceeded as he intended, Demon would've been alone in the house. He would have worn only a pair of boxers to bed. But in his dream, which curiously mirrored real life, he was fully dressed because he had not bathed. His hunting knife with the six-inch blade was holstered on his hip, right where it should be. He barely had the strength to flip the holster's latch with his thumb, so there was no way he was strong enough to pry the monster's hands from his neck.

He never felt so weak.

And even in his dream, he was terribly sleepy.

A part of him did not want to fight back. Why bother? Things would be much simpler if he gave up. There was no way a weakling like him could defeat this tremendous creature.

But then it struck him. His birth name was *David*. And in the bible, David had slain Goliath.

Demon struck out against the creature. He did not believe his attack was successful, even as the blood rained down on his face. He heard the monster cry out. The claws around his neck loosened, and then they were gone completely. Demon sucked in a great breath of air. At that moment, he understood that he truly had not been able to breathe, in his dream and in real life.

Smiling, he fell back to sleep, grateful that he had vanquished the bogeyman.

Some time later, he awakened again. Vaguely, he was aware that his phone was ringing and vibrating in his pocket. He tried to pull it out, but not only were his fingers slippery, but his hand would not cooperate with the instructions his brain was giving it. He decided that it was unimportant.

He went back to sleep.

He was awakened again. More time had passed. How much? Who could know? Once again, it was his phone that had aroused him. He felt like it had been ringing the whole time. He was almost certain that it had. His fingers weren't as sticky now. They were caked with what may have been dried juice. He managed to open his eyes. As he brought the phone to his face, he recognized the stain on his hand as blood.

Was he still dreaming?

He accepted the call. Zahra was frantic.

"Baby! Are you okay? I need help! Simone tried to drug me. I shot her. I think Cujo's coming after you!"

Demon couldn't shake off the remnants of whatever drug he had in his system, but hearing all of that put a lot of the pieces together. When he responded, his voice was so slurred, he was barely intelligible.

"He did. He came for me. I think he put something in my drink."

"*Baby, where are you? Are you okay?*"

"I'm, I'm okay."

His head swam as he tried to sit up. He couldn't make it all the way, but he managed to prop himself on one elbow. He looked to the left and saw the monster he'd slain. Cujo lie motionless. The hunting knife protruded from the side of his neck. There was so much blood.

He managed to tell her, "I'm, I think he's dead. I don't feel good."

"*Where are you?*" she cried.

"New York."

"I don't know what to do with this body, baby. I wanna come to you, but I can't leave her here."

"Who? What body?"

"*Simone.* She tried to kill me."

"Shit. Baby, I can't really understand what's happening right now. But you need to call Zulu. He can help you."

"I'll call him and tell him to go to you first."

"No. Tell him to come help you. I'm okay."

"Should I call someone else to help you?"

"No. I don't want anyone to know what's going on. I trust Zulu. After he takes care of your problem, y'all can head my way."

"Oh, okay," she panted. "Are you sure Cujo's dead?"

"Yeah. Call Zulu. Hurry. I don't know if anybody's coming to that house today."

"Okay. I love you. I'll call you back."

"I love you too."

He dropped the phone and tried to sit up again. He managed it this time, but he was sure he wouldn't be able to walk or even stand up without stumbling. His eyes returned to his fallen brethren. Part of him hoped this was still a dream.

"*Fuck*," he breathed.

None of this made sense. But as he thought about it, he realized that all of it made sense. The trouble between him and Cujo had been brewing for months. He should've seen this coming a mile away.

CHAPTER THIREEN
THE FINAL CHAPTER
LITTLE TIKE'S

Zahra waited at the tactical point for three hours before Zulu arrived. By then, it was two a.m. During that time, she remained in the kitchen and living room, purposely avoiding the body in the bedroom. She called Demon back a couple of times, but he didn't answer. She knew he was having trouble staying awake, despite the fact that he also shared a safehouse with a dead body. She prayed he was only asleep, rather than the victim of a more disturbing fate. The last time she spoke to him, he told her that he did not feel well.

Zulu didn't ask many questions when he arrived. Zahra told him that Simone had tried to kill her, and she had to defend herself. She could see that this news upset him, but he accepted her version of events.

"Cujo did the same thing to Demon," she reported. "The only difference is, Demon drank whatever they put in our drinks. I've been calling him, but he's not answering. He told me Cujo's dead. I don't know how he managed to do that, but he said he was sure he's dead."

Zulu listened, nodded, and then sighed. "I knew they was having some differences of opinions, but I never thought it would come to this."

"Me neither," Zahra said, her eyes brimming with tears.

"I guess Cujo figured he couldn't get rid of Demon without getting rid of you too," Zulu surmised. "Not sure why he got Simone involved, though."

"He wanted to get us both at the same time," Zahra guessed. "I talked to Simone. She was more aligned with Cujo than she was with Demon. I didn't know they were close, but they were on the same page, as far as where they thought the group was headed."

"Fuck it," Zulu said. "It is what it is." He pulled a pair of work gloves from his back pocket. "Let me take care of this place, and then we'll head to New York."

Zahra nodded. "Okay. Oh, and the car in the garage needs to be torched. It's a long story. The clothes I had on last night are in the backseat. We need to make all of that evidence disappear."

If Zulu was bothered by the extra work, it didn't show. He put the gloves on and headed down the hallway. "She in here?"

"Yeah," Zahra said, following him. "The last bedroom on the right. Let me get some gloves, and I'll help you."

∞ ∞ ∞ ∞ ∞ ∞ ∞

Zulu used a box cutter to remove a good deal of the bloody carpet. They rolled Simone in it like a kolache. After all the murders Zahra had committed, she thought she'd become desensitized to such gruesome acts, but she was not. Despite what had transpired between them, she cared about this woman. She thought Simone deserved a more dignified sendoff to eternity than the one she would receive. They managed to stuff the body, carpet and all, in the back seat of the Charger.

They hit the road at three a.m. Zahra was on high alert as she drove the car Zulu had arrived in, following him as he drove the Charger to a destination of his choosing. The light traffic they encountered on the highway made her skin crawl. If Zulu got pulled over, he'd probably have to shoot the cop that had the misfortune of asking to see his license.

But he didn't get pulled over.

After thirty minutes, he exited the freeway. Zahra followed him down a county road. After a few more turns, they arrived in a deserted, wooded area with no nearby homes or streetlights. They poured so much gasoline in the backseat of the Charger, it sounded like a small bomb had gone off when they ignited it. They fled the scene, hoping the darkness would conceal the smoke until sunrise. By then, the woman Zahra had worked with on two missions would be nearly cremated.

She called Demon again, as Zulu drove directly from the fire to the airport. This time he answered.

"Hey, baby."

He sounded a little groggy, but not nearly as bad as the last time she talked to him. Hearing his voice made everything much more bearable.

She asked him, "Are you feeling better?"

"Yeah. I got a bad headache. I feel drunk *and* high, but I don't wanna go back to sleep. I got a lot of work to do here."

"You should get some rest," she told him. "Me and Zulu took care of our issue. We have to get somebody to come lay carpet at the tac point, but we're headed to the airport now. We can help you when we get there."

"Okay. I'll get in touch with Head in a little bit. He can get some people to take care of the carpet. I'm gonna need the same work over here."

"What about the blood?" Zahra asked. "Should we try to clean it up first?"

"No. Don't worry about it. The people I have in mind are discreet. As long as there's no body, they'll keep their mouths shut and do their job."

"What are you gonna tell Head?" she wondered.

"I haven't decided yet. I been sitting here thinking about everything. I can't believe this happened. I can see Cujo coming after me, but you didn't have anything to do with it. And for him to get Simone involved..."

"That's what I was thinking too. Me and her didn't have any problems."

He sighed. "Oh well. They both dead, so I guess we'll never know."

Zahra nodded at how aligned their thinking was.

"I'll come up with something to tell the group," he said. "Everybody respected Cujo. We gotta be careful with this. I'll see y'all in a little bit."

∞ ∞ ∞ ∞ ∞ ∞ ∞

Three days later, the New York and Miami tactical points were back to operational conditions. Demon performed the final walkthrough of the properties personally, to ensure that all evidence of the murders had been concealed. Unless he made it known, no one would ever know what had occurred there.

He left New York and returned to the Houston Headquarters. Once there, he headed for the computer room. He closed the door and spoke to the brains of the operation in a hushed tone. Upon hearing what had occurred, Head and Einstein expressed the same disbelief Demon was grappling with.

"I knew y'all didn't get along," Head said, "but I never thought he'd take it as far as trying to kill you." Shock had given his skin an ashen tone.

"Shit man," Einstein moaned. "This is crazy. And Simone – she was a good soldier. How she get wrapped up in it?"

"I don't know," Demon replied. "But it was her choice, so don't feel too bad for her. She made her bed."

"Cleo's okay?" Head asked. "How's she dealing with all of this?"

"Same as me," Demon said. "We both shook the hell up."

"What are we gonna tell the group?" Einstein wondered.

"That's what I wanted to talk to y'all about," Demon said. "I'm gonna tell them that after our last meeting, Cujo and Simone decided they wanted out. I'll tell them that I respected their decisions and gave them their retirement packages."

"People might believe that about Simone," Einstein stated. "But Cujo? That would be like if Cujo told them *you* decided to leave the group. They'll probably think something's up."

"Maybe," Demon agreed. "But what choice do we have? I can't tell them what went down. And the way me and Cujo been going at it, I think most of 'em know he wasn't happy. Think about it. After the last argument we had in here, if Cujo told us he didn't want to be a part of this anymore, would either of you have been surprised?"

They considered that and shook their heads.

"When we send the message," Demon went on, "I wanna give everybody another opportunity to bow out if they want to."

"*Message*?" Einstein said. "You not calling a meeting for this?"

Demon shook his head. "No. I'm not feeling all that exposure. You saw how cramped it was in here last time. We added a dozen new people since then. We can't keep operating like we used to, having all of us in one place at one time. Plus, if they all come here, they gon' start asking questions I don't have the answers to. And then they gon' start gossiping with each other. I ain't feeling that."

"I get you," Einstein said. "But we just lost one of the founders of the group. A lot of people are gonna feel some type of way."

"That's exactly why they shouldn't come here," Demon argued. "We don't need them expressing those emotions in a group setting. I'm telling y'all, we need to start operating differently. We're soldiers. All of those bitch fests we used to have died with Cujo. We not doing that anymore."

"Alright," Einstein conceded. "When are you sending the message?"

"I want you to send it. You already have the group text set up with their most recent numbers. You can type it up now."

"Okay," Einstein said. He grabbed his phone. When he was ready, he asked, "What do you want me to write?"

"After our last meeting," Demon dictated, "two members chose to leave our organization. One of these members is Cujo. He is officially retired and off the radar. If you would like to join him in retirement, you are welcome to do so. Please respond, if this applies to you."

When he was done typing, Einstein said, "That's it?"

Demon nodded. "Yeah. Lemme see."

Einstein gave him the phone. Demon read it over and then hit Send. He returned the phone to his friend.

"Now what?" Einstein asked.

Demon shrugged. "You can sit there waiting to see if anybody responds. But I gotta bounce. I'm headed to North Carolina. Listen, I know things seem messed up right now, but we gon' be alright. We'll get past this. I appreciate everything y'all do."

He rose from his seat and patted both men on the shoulder before leaving the room.

∞ ∞ ∞ ∞ ∞ ∞ ∞

Demon may have been okay with his plan to proceed as normal, but Zahra had her own concerns. Her boyfriend's plan left one particular rock unturned. Three days after he sent the message, which resulted in one member indicating they were ready to retire, Zahra ran into Einstein on the steps of Little Tikes Daycare. She was exiting the building as he was entering. It was a bright, beautiful afternoon. The look on Einstein's face when he saw her was priceless.

Stunned, he looked her up and down before asking, "Cleo, what are you doing here?"

"I know, right," she said with a smile. "We never see each other out in the open like this. I think this is the first time."

He didn't respond to that.

She said, "Is that your car over there? Let's sit down for a second and have a talk."

Einstein hadn't recovered from the shock of seeing her there. He looked past her at the daycare's entrance. If it wasn't for his dark skin, she was sure he would've gone completely pale.

"Come on," she said, walking past him. "Let's go to your car."

He reluctantly turned and followed her. She looked back at him and thought he looked like a robot; he was moving so stiffly.

She approached the car and waited for him to unlock it. He caught up with her and pressed the button on his key fob. They both got in, him behind the wheel, her on the passenger side. She brought her purse to her lap and slipped her hand inside. She watched him the whole time. His eyes moved from her purse to her face. He was visibly trembling. She could tell he didn't want to close his door, but he did it anyway.

"What, what's going on, Cleo? What are you doing here?"

"Came to check on you," she said, looking around. "Wanted to see how things are going in your world. I know you think Demon is the king of surveillance, but since I started recruiting, I got pretty good at it too. You'd be surprised how much you can learn about somebody by following them around. I knew you had a life outside of our group, but I didn't know you had a little one. A little *tike*," she said, smiling. "What is she, about two and a half?"

His breath came in shudders. "Cleo, please tell me what's going on. Why are you doing this? Demon sent you?"

"No." She shook her head, her smile gone now. "He doesn't know I'm here. I came to see you because I'm protective. Same way you are with certain things, like your computer and your daughter. I don't like it when people come for something I care about. That makes me very angry."

His grimace intensified. "Cleo, I never did anything to you. I don't know what this is about."

"This is about what Cujo did to Demon," she explained. "Here's what I know: You and Cujo been friends for years. You told Cujo you didn't want to help Demon make the *Strange Fruit* video. You got pissed when the hackers started targeting you after Demon gave the orders to take down the militia. And when it was time for Cujo to make his move, he just happened to know Demon would be in New York. How'd he know? Oh, that would be you again. You told Cujo where he could find Demon that night."

"Cleo, those are all coincidences. Yes, Cujo asked me where Demon would be, but I didn't think anything crazy was gonna happen. Cujo asks me stuff like that all the time. Demon never told me not to tell anyone about his location." He was near tears.

"I figured you'd say that. You want me to believe you had nothing to do with it, and you don't have a problem with Demon."

"I don't. I'm telling you the truth!"

"Maybe," Zahra said. "I'm not positive about what I've been worried about. If I was, you never would've seen me coming." She removed her hand from her purse. "I hope you understand why I had to come at you like this. I can't let anything happen to Demon. If you had nothing to do with what Cujo did, then I hope we can move on from this with no hard feelings."

He nodded anxiously. "Yeah. We can. I'm sorry for telling Cujo where Demon was that night. I swear I didn't know what he was gonna do."

She watched his eyes and was sure he was telling the truth. She told him, "In the future, I need you to operate with the understanding that things may not always be as they seem. Just because only one person said they wanted to leave the group doesn't mean everybody else is happy.

"You and Head are in contact with our members more than anyone else. When you hear people complaining about an issue they have with Demon, and these same people ask you where he's gonna be on a particular date and time, you need to let me know *before* you give out that information. *I'll* let you know how to respond to them. From now on, I'm responsible for Demon's security."

"Okay. I will. I promise."

"Don't forget how they got Fred Hampton. A member of his own group drugged him, set him up for the police to kill him. Throughout our history, most groups like ours have been taken down from within."

Einstein nodded, his mood somber. "Yeah, I know."

She looked back at the daycare and then met his eyes again before opening the door and exiting the vehicle.

"Try to enjoy the rest of your day. Go get your daughter. She's a cutie."

EPILOGUE

According to her children, Shirley Baker was too young to be as engrossed with knitting as she was. She'd taken up the hobby after her divorce. Her therapist suggested that she find a hobby that was relaxing, something just for her that could pull her attention away from the thought of her ex-husband screwing another woman. The divorce had been contentious. George got entangled in a salacious affair with his busty secretary (*how cliché!*), and they continued the relationship after Shirley mustered the fortitude to kick him out of the house.

Putting him out had been a last resort. She'd hoped he'd crawl back to her on his hands and knees. She would have forgiven him. She would've put him in the doghouse for a few months, but over time, they could've worked to heal their marriage. Instead, George picked option B. The asshole chose to leave his wife for a woman half his age. For the life of her, Shirley couldn't understand what the floozy saw in George, but she certainly understood what he saw in her. The secretary had legs for days, perky boobs, long, blonde hair.

Shirley, on the other hand, was not attractive. Her boobs hadn't been perky in decades, and at 52, she had jowls that were starting to make her look like a hound dog. The likelihood of her finding a man who would love her as much as George once had was slim to none. And with the children living their lives in other parts of the city, her home was no longer a home – not with George gone. It was simply a *house* now, a house that grew more cold and desolate by the day.

Knitting took her mind off these things. Since taking up the habit, she'd knitted a dozen scarves, bibs for her grandbabies. She was now ready to move on to gloves and more complicated patterns. On Saturday afternoon, she went to her favorite store, Hobby Lobby, in search of the necessary supplies. As she pushed her buggy down brightly lit aisles that were filled with eccentric goodies, she realized she was being followed.

Actually, *targeted* was the word that came to mind.

The culprit was a black man (no surprise there), who looked completely out of place in the establishment. He wore an Adidas jumpsuit with sneakers. He looked to be in his mid to late twenties. He had a moustache and a tuft of hair on his chin. His hair was shaved low on the sides with more left on the top. Shirley didn't have to know him to know that he was not a knitter. She doubted if any other item in the store was of interest to him. He was not the type of man who entertained himself with hobbies. He was also not the type of man who would own a home, so she doubted if he was checking out the decorative pieces sold at the store.

No, what this man was interested in was *crime.* That was his hobby. That's why he wore an outfit that would make it easy to run away after he snatched a hardworking woman's purse. Shirley had a gift, when it came to figuring people out. She could piece together a person's whole life in a matter of seconds. The black man had three children out of wedlock. He had been to prison. He used drugs. He was currently on parole. He was armed and dangerous. Shirley knew all of this as well as she knew her own name.

Despite the violence this man was capable of, she was not afraid of him. In America, there are rules of decorum, and there are laws put in place to protect people like her from certain black people. After spotting him on the same aisle she just happened to be on for a third time, she girded herself for the confrontation and then initiated it.

She walked right up to him and asked, "Excuse me, do you need help finding something?"

He immediately sneered at her. "What?" he spat.

She looked up at him, her eyes as poisonous as his. "I said do you need help finding something?"

"Do you work here?"

"No, I do not."

"Then why you asking me if I need help? You need to mind your business."

Shirley's privilege gave her the courage to stand her ground. "I'm asking if you need help because you've been following me around this store. If you're trying to buy the same things I'm buying, maybe I can help you find it."

With his teeth bared, he said, "Bitch, if you don't get the fuck out my face, I'ma slap the shit outta you."

Shirley's eyes flashed open wide as she gasped. Reaching into her purse, she said, "I'm calling the police."

"For what?"

"You just threatened me!"

"You the one messing with me!"

She had her phone out by then. She placed the call. The man shook his head and retreated.

"I can't stand y'all motherfuckers. Always calling the police on somebody..."

Shirley watched him walk away as the call was answered.

"911, what's your emergency?"

"A man just threatened me," she said. Her voice was as flustered as she felt. Her tears squirted easily. "I'm at the Hobby Lobby on Preston Road." She gave the woman the address.

"Okay, how were you threatened, ma'am?"

"A black man was following me around," she blubbered. "I just, I asked him if he needed help finding anything. And he, and he, he said he'd *slap the shit out of me.* He said that, right in front of everybody. *Please send help!*"

By then the commotion had drawn the attention of a few customers and a store employee. They hurried to her aisle.

The employee asked, "What happened? What's wrong?"

"Is the man still there?" the operator asked.

"No, he left," Shirley cried. "There are people here. *Everybody saw it!*"

"Do you need me to send the police?" the operator asked. "Could you ask the manager of the store to check to see if the man is still there?"

"Did you see which way that man went?" Shirley asked the employee.

"What man?"

"*The black guy.* He's wearing an Adidas jumpsuit. He was right here a second ago."

Shirley was red about the face. Her hand trembled. The employee was in his late teens. He was concerned but ill-equipped to handle a crisis of this magnitude.

"I'm, I'll go check," he said and hurried off.

"He's going to check," Shirley told the operator. "Oh my God, *I'm so scared.* I thought he was going to kill me." She placed her free hand on her chest. She could feel her heart rattling.

"Okay," the operator said. "Stay on the phone with me. When the manager returns, let me speak to him."

"That wasn't, I don't think that was the manager. But I'm headed to the front now."

"Okay. Try to calm down," the operator said. "It sounds like the man is no longer there. But if he is, I'll send the police."

"Okay. Thank you so much. I'm so scared. He was going to kill me..."

∞ ∞ ∞ ∞ ∞ ∞ ∞

She called 911 again thirty minutes later.

The first operator did not send the police to the store. At the time, Shirley understood why they chose not to do so. The man who had verbally assaulted her was no longer in the store or in the parking lot. He most likely took off on foot. The store manager apologized profusely for what had happened. But with the assailant no longer available to arrest or even question, there was no action the police could take.

While driving home, Shirley's mind continued to race. She didn't notice when a car pulled alongside her and maintained the same speed for several blocks. After failing to get her attention with his mere presence, the driver of the other vehicle honked his horn. Shirley looked to the left and was shocked to see the same man from Hobby Lobby. When he was sure he had her attention, he flipped her off and shouted an obscenity. With his windows up and hers up as well, she couldn't hear what he said, but she read his lips perfectly. His threat matched his hand gesture.

"Fuck you!"

With her Bluetooth enabled, the 911 operator's voice resonated through her car's speakers.

"911, what's your emergency?"

"*Help me! I'm being followed! There's a man following me and threatening me!*"

"Okay, ma'am. What's your name?"

"*Shirley Baker.* I called earlier about this man! He threatened me in Hobby Lobby, and now he's following me!"

As she spoke, the other car sped up.

"*He's getting away!*" she shrieked. "He's, I can't–
"

"Calm down, ma'am. What's your location?"

"I'm driving. I'm going east on Beltline. I'm coming up on Coit."

"What did the man do to threaten you?"

"He yelled at me. He said *fuck you!*"

"He said this from the side of the road?"

"No! *He's driving.* He's in a car, a black Charger. He pulled up next to me and cursed me out! *He's getting away! I don't see him anymore!*"

"You said he's following you?"

"Yes! I called when he threatened me at Hobby Lobby. And now I see him again on the street. *It's the same man!*"

"How is he following you, if he's getting away?"

"He just drove off! Aren't you listening? He drove up next to me and cursed at me, and then he drove off!"

"Well, ma'am, if he drove off, why do you think he's following you?"

"Because it's the *same black guy* from Hobby Lobby!" She resisted the urge to call the operator an idiot.

"Okay, ma'am, please try to remain calm."

"Don't tell me to remain calm!"

"Alright. I found the record of your call thirty minutes ago. It says a man cursed at you while you were at Hobby Lobby."

"Yes, this is the same person!"

"Is it possible that you just happened to see him again when you left the store, and he's upset because of what happened earlier? What did he do to threaten you while you were in your car?"

"He drove up next to me and said *fuck you!*"

"Okay. Is that all he did?"

Shirley was incredulous. "What do you mean is that all? That's not enough?"

"I understand that it does not feel good to be cursed at, but it doesn't sound like this man is *threatening* you. At most, this falls under *disorderly conduct.* You're welcome to file a police report, but this is not an emergent situation, especially if the man is not following you."

"You want me to file a police report when I'm telling you I'm being followed?" Shirley snapped angrily.

"You said he drove off..."

Shirley could tell by the voice that this operator was a black woman. "A lot of good you people are!" she said and disconnected.

∞ ∞ ∞ ∞ ∞ ∞ ∞

She called 911 a third time at 10:13 p.m. This time there was no mistaking the validity of the emergency. Someone was breaking into her home. She heard the glass break on her patio door. Panicked, she ran to her bedroom and hid in the closet. Eyes wide, breaths coming in ragged shudders, she placed the call.

"911, what's your emergency?"

"*I need help,*" she whispered. "*Someone's breaking into my house. Please send somebody now. Please.*"

"Okay, ma'am. What's your address."

She gave the operator the information.

"What's your name?"

"Shirley Baker. Oh, my God. Please send somebody fast. I can hear them. *They're in my house.*"

"Help is on the way, Mrs. Baker. Try to calm down."

"I can't. I'm scared. Oh, I'm so scared."

"Hey, didn't you call 911 two times already today?" the operator asked.

Stunned, she asked, "What does that have to do with anything?" She heard footsteps downstairs.

"I'm just saying," the operator said. "You called the police when somebody cursed at you at Hobby Lobby, and you called again when they cursed you out on the street."

"Please, just, I don't – what are you talking about?"

"A pattern of behavior," the operator said. "Isn't that what they established during your civil trial? The plaintiff proved that you have a pattern of behavior when it comes to making 911 calls. In the past three years, you called 911 *forty-five times*, forty-eight, if we count the calls you made today. Nearly all of those calls had to do with you getting into it with a black person."

Civil trial? Black person?

"What? What is, what's going on?"

The footsteps were closer now, headed up the stairs.

"During the trial," the operator continued, "Wayne Allen's family was suing you for your role in the circumstances that led to his death. Sure, it was the police who beat and choked him. But the police wouldn't have been there if you hadn't called them. Wayne was panhandling in the parking lot. You called 911 and said he threatened you. Isn't that right?"

"What are you talking about? What does that have to do with people breaking into my house *right now*? *I need help!*"

"Yes," the operator said. "You do need help. You're in big trouble now. But the reason you're in trouble goes back to what happened to *Wayne*. You called the police on him just like you call the police on damn near every black person that looks at you the wrong way. That makes you a *Karen*, Shirley. You beat the civil trial, but the plaintiffs proved that you're a Karen. You like to sic the cops on black people.

"After what happened to Wayne, and what's been going on across this country, you are fully aware that sometimes when the cops show up, they take it too far. They beat that man to death right in front of you. But did that stop you? Nope. Since Wayne's death, you've called the police on *ten more black people*. That's not counting today."

Sobbing, Shirley said, "*I don't know what you want from me. Please stop...*"

"What I want," the operator (who was also known as Einstein) said, "is for white bitches like you to stop calling the police on black people who haven't done anything but look suspicious. It's too late for you, but I'm hoping that after what happens tonight, other Karens will think twice before they continue down the same path as you."

"*What do you mean it's too late for me?*" she cried.

"It's too late for you to change," Einstein stated. "Them niggas is in yo house. They gon' get you. Before they take care of business, do me a favor: Spend your last few moments thinking about Wayne and all the other black people you tried to get the police to kill."

The phone went dead in Shirley's ear.

The closet door opened.

She saw two figures wearing all black, their faces obscured by ski masks. She never saw the guns, but she felt the first bullets hit her.

As they made a smooth getaway, Zahra asked Demon, "When is Einstein gonna send the audio from those 911 calls? I can't wait to hear 'em."

Demon grinned. "We'll get 'em tonight. I can't wait, either. You know, I don't think I ever had fun with our jobs – I mean, I enjoy all of 'em, but as far as having legit *fun* while carrying them out, I never felt that before – until today. I had a good time with that bitch."

Chuckling, Zahra said, "I know you did! You got to show off your acting skills."

"I wasn't even acting, though. I responded to her the same way any black man in that position would've responded."

"We should make a video of those 911 calls."

"Oh, you got jokes."

"No, seriously. If we wanna put out a strong message, that would make it hit home."

"No doubt," he said, nodding. "I assume you wanna let the group vote on it before we do something like that..."

She surprised him by saying, "Nope. We don't need permission to do the right thing. Fuck who don't like it."

Laughing, he said, "Damn. I created a monster."

"A *demon*. A lady demon."

"That makes you a *succubus*."

She thought about that and said, "Nah, I like lady demon better."

"For sure," he said nodding.

Thirty minutes later, they had left Dallas city limits, headed to the Houston headquarters. After a restful night's sleep, they planned to take separate flights in the morning to cities on opposite coasts.

There was always much work to do.

KEITH THOMAS WALKER

ABOUT THE AUTHOR

Keith Thomas Walker, known as the Master of Romantic Suspense and Urban Fiction, is the author of more than two dozen novels, including *Fixin' Tyrone, Life After, The Realest Ever,* the *Backslide* series, the *Brick House* series, the *Finley High* series and the *Asha and Boom* series. Keith's books transcend all genres. He has published romance, urban fiction, mystery/thriller, teen/young adult, Christian, poetry and erotica. Originally from Fort Worth, he is a graduate of Texas Wesleyan University. Keith has won numerous awards in the categories of "Best Male Author," "Best Romance," "Best Urban Fiction," "Best Young Adult Romance," "Best Duo," "Book of the Year," and "Author of the Year," from several book clubs and organizations. Visit him at www.keithwalkerbooks.com.

CPSIA information can be obtained
at www.ICGtesting.com
Printed in the USA
JSHW022026240523
42207JS00001B/65